DIARY OF A FAIRY PRINCESS

 • DEVIANT MAGIC • BOOK THREE

Scott Colby

DEVIANT MAGIC BOOK THREE: DIARY OF A FAIRY PRINCESS
Copyright © 2021 Scott Colby. All rights reserved.

Published by Outland Entertainment LLC
3119 Gillham Road
Kansas City, MO 64109

Founder/Creative Director: Jeremy D. Mohler
Editor-in-Chief: Alana Joli Abbott

ISBN: 978-1-954255-02-9
EBOOK ISBN: 978-1-954255-03-6
Worldwide Rights
Created in the United States of America

Editor: Gwendolyn N. Nix
Cover Illustration: Ann Marie Cochran
Cover Design: Jeremy D. Mohler
Interior Layout: Mikael Brodu

Printed and bound in the United States of America.

Visit **outlandentertainment.com** to see more, or follow us on our Facebook Page **facebook.com/outlandentertainment/**

— CHAPTER ONE —

This is the worst hiding place ever," Myrindi snapped with the sort of melodramatic huff only a spoiled teenaged girl can manage. "You assholes suck at this rescue shit."

"Take it easy, Princess," Lep said soothingly. A big bear of a man, the elf's head almost scraped the low stone ceiling of the ancient storage room they'd ducked into. "We'll be safe here."

Her dark eyes narrowed and her blue cheeks flushed purple. "Why can't we be safe somewhere with some natural light? My tan's going to go straight to hell in this hole and vitamin D deficiencies have always been hell on my mood."

"But you don't really tan, you navy blue," Lep replied, his beefy jowls quivering. "And you're safe."

"My stylist warned me that prolonged exposure to cold, damp places could lead to discoloration of my highlights."

"But you're *safe*. And you're a water nymph. Cold and damp is your natural habitat."

"And how can I *possibly* keep up with the Kardashians without a television? Kanye's new single drops tomorrow."

"But you're safe."

"And I was supposed to be at Tachel's sweet sixteen half an hour ago—"

"Shut the fuck up!" Pike roared, stepping between the two of them. Although not nearly as enormous as Lep, Pike nonetheless was large enough and in good enough shape that most people wouldn't want to mess with him. His plate armor shone the color of fresh blood in the soft light thrown by the single flickering halogen in the corner. A huge broadsword was strapped to his back. "And you, Lep, I don't know what kind of perverse pleasure you get from riling up this little bitch—"

"Little bitch?" Thin as a rail, Myrindi shifted her weight back onto her heels, stuck one bony hip out to the side, and crossed her arms over her chest. The simple white shift she wore hung loosely from her narrow shoulders. The gills in the sides of her slender neck fluttered angrily. "Little bitch? Do you know what happened to the last Rot-licking asshole who spoke to me that way?"

Pike rubbed the top of his shaved head as he considered her question. "Absolutely nothing."

Myrindi squinted right back at the burly elf. "Fine. Technically, you're right. But that guy's on my list and he *will* get his."

From her seat beside the tiny room's only door—a hunk of dented metal that had seen better days and much better paint jobs—Chastity cleared her throat loudly. A pretty young woman with bright red hair and pale skin spattered with freckles, she was dressed conservatively in sandals, a pair of ripped blue jeans, and a gray T-shirt sporting the Irish flag. She looked more like a tourist on holiday than a commando on a rescue mission. "Hey, you know what's kind of hard? Maintaining a magically cloaked door while a bunch of dumbasses argue about stupid shit like a bunch of five-year-olds kicking dirt at each other on the damn playground."

Pike took a step closer to the tiny princess and stuck his finger in her face. "Exactly. So if you don't shut your trap, I'll shut it for you."

A shadow detached itself from the wall, taking the shape of a gnarled old troll as it inserted itself between Pike and Myrindi. "You shall not threaten the Princess," Froman growled, his deep voice seeming to fill all the empty space in the small room. Knobs and warts and whorls pocked his scaly, yellowish-green skin. Under a loose black robe typically stocked with all manner of tools, weapons, and supplies, he wore a black chainmail shirt over black jeans with a pair of combat boots.

Pike glared down his nose at Myrindi's protector. He had a couple inches on the troll, but Froman outweighed him by a good hundred pounds. "Keep her quiet."

Froman let his angry gaze linger on Pike one moment longer, then he took the princess's elbow and led her to the back corner. "He's an ass, but he's right. The more noise we make, the greater our chances of being discovered," he explained gently as he motioned for Myrindi to take a seat atop a short pile of wooden pallets.

She wrinkled her little nose at the offered seat, but she sat nonetheless. Her sore legs needed a break. She figured she'd done enough running that day to keep her personal trainer off her back for at least a week or two.

"I'm going to go stir crazy in here, Fro," Myrindi whined. "Developing young minds like mine require appropriate stimulation. I can't believe I let you talk me into leaving without my tablet."

"I've got something even better than that infernal device," Froman replied happily. His wide smile transformed him from a rugged, untamed beast to a cartoon ogre ready to burst into song. He reached inside his robe and produced a leather-bound journal. "I grabbed this before we fled your chambers. Thought you might want it."

With a mighty sigh and an eye roll that would've made most observers immediately dizzy, Myrindi snatched the journal and opened it up to its first page. "Fine."

Dear Dumb Fucking Diary,

I can't believe I've been reduced to writing my life's story in the back corner of a janitor's supply closet. In case you haven't heard, I'm Myrindi XVII, Crown Princess of Talvayne, and I do not often frequent dirty, dingy places like the one in which I now find myself trapped. A janitor's closet is for mops and buckets and poor people who want to fornicate when they're supposed to be at work.

And as for you, Diary, suffice to say that you and I wouldn't be spending this quality time together had I entertainment options beyond reading the labels of various cleaning supplies, counting cockroaches, or giving Pike the Royal Stink Eye when he isn't looking. I've avoided you for thirteen years, after all, so don't you start thinking we're friends all of a sudden. We're just temporary acquaintances, kind of like people matched on dating shows. Fro gave you to me on my third birthday. Apparently it's tradition for Talvayan Crown Princesses to keep a journal no one else ever reads. Fuck that noise. You are kind of cool, though. This whole "think about what you want to write and the words just appear" thing would've been super useful during my penmanship lessons. Learning cursive never helped anybody.

But that's enough about you, Diary. I'm the star of this here memoir; you're just part of the supporting cast. I'd put you on the marquee just below Fro but way, way above Pike. Take a powder. And get some lotion. You're looking a bit chapped.

In medias res openings have always seemed a bit cheeky to me, so the inspirational, heartwarming, perfectly written story of my life will start at the only logical place: the very beginning. As the cells of my little fetus brain flared to life, I couldn't help being struck by how fucking pink my surroundings were. Mother's uterus really needed an interior decorator—and a thermostat. It was like a troll's armpit in there, except it smelled a little better. Sorry, Fro.

I spent the ensuing four months floating, absorbing nutrients, and listening. There was a whole world beyond my dark, poorly decorated prison, and it was full of loud, obnoxious ass-hats. Most of Mother's time was spent listening to the inane requests of bitchy people who needed more room for their goats, less noise out of their neighbors, or the continued support of the crown in bringing their experimental cheese-based geomancy project to fruition. Mother rarely replied to these petitions, leaving Father to do the majority of the work—and make the final decision, which struck me as a bit odd. Why bother putting Mother through all that if she couldn't really contribute? I got the general impression that she was just an accessory, a pretty pair of earrings stuck crookedly into the gangrenous ears of a governmental apparatus that thought it was the coolest cat on the block but in reality didn't have a clue how tragically unhip it really was.

Sorry about that, Diary. Didn't mean to go all nerd-burgers on you. I'll tone it back down.

There were also lots of what I would later learn to be parties. At the time, I had no clue what Mother had wandered into. What the Rot was all that noise and fuss and hullabaloo? The rare people who stopped being ridiculous for a few moments to offer their congratulations or a few words of encouragement confused me even more. Mother was saddled with a great responsibility, apparently, and she was fulfilling it with the grace and dignity befitting someone of her station. Maybe she'd been named den mother of a troop of pretentious girl scouts. Maybe it was her job to guard the nuclear football. Maybe it was something as simple as cleaning the pool or sweeping the stairs. No one explicitly said, so I had no clue that yours truly was actually the reason for all the chatter. Ah, to be that young and naïve again...would actually suck sweaty elf taint, come to think of it.

Sometimes the outside was quiet. These times were exceedingly rare, but Mother put each and every one of them to good use. When no one else was around, her soft, scratchy voice worked a mile a minute as she described the world and her role in it. She told me about being princess and becoming queen and knowing her death wasn't far off. She told me about Talvayne, our home. She told me about the deadly Rot surrounding the city and the magical network of transpoints that connects us to the rest of the planet. She told me about the billions and billions of humans and the sorcery used to keep them oblivious to the existence of fairy folk like us. I committed every single syllable to memory, reciting them to myself when the outside became too raucous for my tender little ears to deal with.

And then, after months of unbearable warmth in the unfurnished efficiency unit that was Mother's womb, my birthday finally came. Mother's insides quivered like a teenaged pop star loaded up on cough syrup cocktails. I knew it was time for me to be born, but I would've held onto something had I known exactly what that entailed. As I was shoved violently out into the world through the fleshy canopy of Mother's woo-woo, a single cry burst forth from my lips.

"What the fucking fuck?"

It was too bright. It was too cold. My brain was far too addled to focus on anything. Mother was crying. And—worst of all—some stranger had his hand on my ass.

"Put me down, you plebeian neanderthal!" I roared.

"Congratulations, Your Highness," the stranger said as he offered me to Father. "A beautiful new Talvayan Crown Princess!"

"The man's got good taste, but he's copping waaaaaaay too much of a feel," I added.

"Yes, yes," Father replied as he deftly avoided the doctor's attempt to hand me off. Lard Ass is not the type of man to hold angry, sticky newborns. "See that she's cleaned up and vaccinated and all that. The nanny will take care of the rest."

"Yes, Your Highness."

The doctor set me down gently on something soft and absorbent. As my eyes adjusted to the harsh fluorescent light of the birthing room, I suddenly found myself face-to-face for the first time—and the only time—with my mother. She was beautiful, both for a wood nymph and for someone covered in sweat and leaking blood from all her orifices. But still. She was a perfect angel, a petite beauty with girl-next-door good looks carved in wooden skin and trimmed in leafy green hair. When our eyes met...well, that's the only time I've ever cried. Seriously. I fucking swear. I was just pretending all the other times. Fuck you, Diary.

"I love you, Myrindi," she muttered as she breathed her last breath.

"Love you too, Mother," I wailed, "but I was really hoping you'd name me River or Bailey or Zoe or something a little more modern and hip, you know. Mother? Mother!"

She'd been telling me for days that she would die delivering me, that it was just the way life goes when you're Queen of Talvayne, but I hadn't believed her. It sounded too horrible to be true. I'd hoped Mother was just nervous and scared and too caught up on the worst-case scenario. I'd been wrong, and it made me wish I'd spent more time with her—you know, even though I'd technically never *not* been with her. I just always assumed we'd have all the time in the world to be best pals. Nope. My mother was dead.

And Lard Ass hadn't even said good-bye. Thought I'd point that out in case you needed further proof that he's a total tool shed.

— CHAPTER TWO —

Breathing a mighty sigh, Myrindi stood up and stretched. The stack of pallets on which she'd been sitting wasn't doing her posture any favors, but she had a much more immediate need to address. With an agile leap over the poker game Pike and Lep had laid out on the floor, she approached Chastity, who still sat against the room's only door. The red-haired woman smiled and motioned for the princess to sit beside her.

"Pssst," Myrindi hissed conspiratorially as she knelt down. "Girl talk."

Chastity leaned forward to return Myrindi's whisper. "What's up?"

The princess hesitated. The only other occasion on which she'd talked with a demon had turned into a total clusterfuck. Chastity looked human on the outside, but the magic Myrindi had seen her use meant she could only be one thing. "I have to... erm...powder my nose."

"Plenty of buckets in here."

"My Royal Lady Water does not belong in a bucket crawling with common filth!" Myrindi snapped a little louder than she had intended. Behind her, Pike chuckled.

"So what do you want from me?" Chastity asked. "I'm fresh out of hall passes. Must be a Royal Piss Bucket on one of these shelves, still in the original shrink wrap."

Pike laughed again.

"Oh, hardy-har-har! Don't you feel any sense of camaraderie toward a fellow female? I bet you wouldn't lower yourself to tinkling in a bucket!"

"You're right about that, sugar buns," Chastity replied. "I'm just going to use that corner over there."

"You can pee on me anytime, oh beloved wife-o-mine!" Lep declared merrily.

"Thanks, boo, but this is neither the time nor the place for a golden shower. It'll have to wait until your birthday next month."

"Rats!"

Crossing her arms angrily, Myrindi screwed her pretty little face into an angry pout. "Fine. I'll hold it. Our next hiding place had better include a fully stocked washroom, complete with a lavender-scented bidet and hot towels."

The princess turned on her heel and stomped back toward her pile of pallets in the corner. She stole a look at Pike's cards as she passed.

"Better fold, Lep. This fucker's packing most of that low straight from the flop. Old Man River won't save you on this one."

Lep laid down his hand with a smarmy smile. Pike raked in the pot disgustedly, muttering something unintelligible about haughty little blue bitches.

Dear Diary,

I still remember the first time someone told me "no." I was three years old at the time, a pretty little lass in pigtails and floral print who dragged a raggedy teddy bear named Cliff everywhere she went. Right. If you believe that, I've got a gnoll who smells like roses you just *have* to meet.

Anyway, there I was in my black velvet Dior jumper, my hair freshly highlighted and curled, making sure my father knew that my fourth birthday just wouldn't be right if it didn't include an appearance by Justin Timberlake and at least three elephants. Fro stood patiently behind me as always, a silent sentinel prepared to strike down any and all who might threaten my person.

"Nella had five tigers and Jordan Knight at her tenth birthday last week," I said methodically, reciting the sales pitch I'd been rehearsing in front of the help for several days. The unique auditory qualities of the throne room's spiraling design amplified my tiny voice without the assistance of either magic or technology. I was miffed that my father's retainers had forgotten to set up the laptop and projector I'd asked for, but I'd decided that the innate power of my argument would not be hindered by a lack of Powerpoint. "She's merely third in line to be matron of House Lucardia. As the one-and-only Crown Princess of Talvayne, I can't afford to be one-upped by some swamp-dwelling trailer trash with a harelip and almost no chance of marrying up. My station demands social superiority. It's a heavy burden, but one I shall carry wherever I must."

Father, his fat blue ass planted firmly on the Throne of Light, didn't deign to look up from his crossword puzzle. He barely fit in that chair. It's thousands of years old and glitters all the colors of the rainbow, even in the dark. It's supposed to represent the king's power over Talvayne's diverse population or something dorky like that. I wondered if anyone would know how to expand the thing if Father got too big to sit in it. Dude was built like Humpty-Dumpty, round and wide and sort of impossible looking. Water nymphs like the two of us are typically small, wispy things that might blow away in a strong enough breeze, which made his girth all the more impressive and confusing. His scraggly gray mustache and matching middle manager combover both needed to go. I'm pretty sure the red and gold robes he favored were typically sold as tents in the local sporting goods store. As usual, he'd gone crown-less that day. He preferred to save the fancy hardware for special occasions because he claimed it made his scalp itch.

Frustrated with my father's lack of a response, I looked to his captain of the guard and personal protector, a hulking, twisted troll named Gaptorix. Unlike the rest of his men, Gaptorix refuses to wear armor, believing instead that a true warrior doesn't need any protection beyond the weapon in his hand—which in Gaptorix's case is a nasty black axe he carries around like a security blanket. The only thing he wears is a ragged loincloth which makes it quite clear his entire act is just compensating for a certain something. Scars crisscross his rough yellow skin, transforming his broad chest into something roughly equivalent to the sole of a leather shoe that should've been thrown out years ago. He looks like he'd been hit in the face repeatedly. It's not a good look, but he'd rebuked all of my attempts to give him a proper makeover. Not that I could've done much to really help the poor guy. No matter how many coats of paint you put on an outhouse, it's still an outhouse, right? Anyway, one of the best ways to get Lard Ass's attention was always to pretend someone else was really in charge— especially if that someone was his captain of the guard.

"Gaptorix, what do you think?" I chirped. "Sounds like an appropriate celebration to me."

That did it. Father glared down at me briefly and then went back to his puzzle. "No."

I couldn't believe my ears, but I was undeterred. My mother had spent the majority of her pregnancy drilling the necessity of getting my way and asserting my importance into my receptive young psyche. I was ready for a fight. "I don't think you understand the sociopolitical ramifications of your decision, Father," I countered.

"I understand that you are a little girl about to turn four," Lard Ass rumbled, the jowls on his jowls quivering like a gelatin mold being carried down a steep flight of stairs by a servant with a peg leg. Supposedly he was quite handsome in his younger years. You could see a strong chin and an aquiline nose under there, but just barely. "How do you even know who Justin Timberlake is?"

"The maids watch MTV for me and report back every Saturday at two," I explained. "How else?" I mean, just because the humans don't know we magic fairy people even exist doesn't mean I shouldn't keep up with what they think is hot. They drive the vast majority of the world's culture, after all. It's their chief export.

My father's face flushed as if the buffet had just closed an hour early. "You should be watching cartoons that teach you how to spell!"

"Duh, that's why I have the maids performing cultural recon. I'm not getting into Berkeley if I let basic cable rot my impressionable young mind."

"If you're so set on your studies, why do you care about this tripe?"

"It's called 'being well-rounded,' Father. Book smarts are no good if I can't also apply my intelligence to real-world situations."

"Talvayan Crown Princesses have no need to be well-rounded," Lard Ass burbled.

"Have you ever been a Talvayan Crown Princess?" I kind of hoped his answer would be in the affirmative, if only so as to add a few layers to his bland character.

"No."

"Then you can't possibly comprehend the pressures inherent to the job."

"I comprehend them better than you, I would think. Enough of this. Your birthday is going to be a small, respectful affair in the Glittering Gardens. Family only. What do you children like on your birthday cakes these days? Ponies? Mermaids?"

A warm, intense feeling bubbled up from deep in the pit of my stomach. At first I thought it was gas, but the sensation quickly established itself as something new and different, something that sucked the life out of the room and left me gasping for breath. Let's see you go almost four whole years without experiencing the rancid taste of utter disappointment and we'll see how well you handle yourself. It's a real shock to the system, like realizing the servants forgot to change your sheets or being handed a vodka tonic when you clearly asked for a dirty martini. I found myself wishing it were uncontrollable, explosive flatulence simply so my father would've also had to deal with the results.

The throne room darkened. It's a round, obnoxiously white space shaped a bit like the interior of a giant traffic cone with a narrow ledge spiraling diagonally up its inside edge. There's a broad glass panel at the top that provides the room's only illumination. That pane gave me a great view of the swath of dark clouds that had gathered above Talvayne. Appropriate, I thought, for what I was about to be reduced to.

Summoning every ounce of fury my mother and her favorite soap opera divas had instilled in my impressionable young mind, I stood up straight, crossed my spindly little arms across my chest, and equally distributed all of my boiling vitriol between my eyes and my tongue. "Ponies and mermaids, Father? *Ponies and mermaids?* This is a princess's birthday party we're talking about here, not some low-rent elven drag show!"

In the distance, thunder rumbled. My father glanced around the room uneasily. "Your mother loved ponies and mermaids when she was your age."

"The hell she did!" Another thunderclap punctuated my protest. "My mother was an educated woman of class and refinement!"

The flash of a nearby lightning bolt briefly lit up the room. "F-fine," Lard Ass capitulated. "Justin Timberlake and two elephants."

I'd originally asked for three, but I decided to push my advantage while I had Father on the ropes. "Four elephants."

"Four," he agreed. "Can't have rain this weekend..."

I smiled smugly, content to enjoy my victory without rubbing it in too deeply. The last thing I needed was to develop a reputation as an unreasonable bitch. "Deal," I declared. "And order some of that strawberry cheesecake you like so much for dessert." Offering someone a hand back up after knocking him down, after all, is the honorable thing to do.

As Fro escorted me away from my defeated father on our way back to my chambers, the clouds outside dissipated and lit the throne room in warm light once more. My intrepid protector hunched down so he could whisper in my ear.

"Remember what I told Your Highness about the Crown Princess's magical bond with Talvayne?" he asked gently.

"Of course. You never shut up about it."

"And does Your Highness understand what happened back there?"

I scratched my chin, considering. Lard Ass had gotten awfully itchy about a potential storm. In fact, he hadn't seemed willing to give in until that lightning strike.

That's when it hit me. "My mood influences the weather."

He nodded sagely. "Very good, Princess, but keep it to yourself. That's not information we typically spread around.

Generations of Talvayan Crown Princesses have grown up, borne a successor, and passed without making that connection—but I think your mother would've wanted you to know."

"Of course she did," I replied, smiling evilly. "She wanted me to be the best Talvayan Crown Princess I can be."

"Indeed she did, Your Highness."

— CHAPTER THREE —

Myrindi looked up from her journal and glanced furtively around the room to make sure her would-be rescuers were suitably occupied. Lep and Pike were focused on their latest hand, studying the flop as if it held the answers to every mystery of the universe. Chastity, meanwhile, sat with the side of her head pressed against the metal door and her eyes shut tight. Either she was asleep or she was concentrating so deeply on maintaining the room's magical protections that she may as well have been. Myrindi didn't really care either way.

The princess flipped to the next blank page in her journal, mentally scribbled a quick line, then tilted the book so Froman, who was seated on the floor beside her, could see it.

Can we trust them?

The troll shrugged. He had no clue. That didn't sit well with Myrindi. She and Fro had followed the other three on the spur of the moment simply because it had seemed smarter than staying in her chambers while Sorrin and his trolls consolidated their control of the palace. The possibility that she was being led into an even worse situation gnawed at the princess.

Pretty much everyone she'd ever met had wanted something from her. So what did Lep, Chastity, and Pike want? Born into a social station that had tried its damnedest to teach her about tact and failed miserably, she decided to just ask.

"Can we trust you?"

Pike and Lep traded confused looks. Chastity's eyes snapped open. Froman, who was used to the princess's forwardness and, truth be told, welcomed it in this particular instance, didn't so much as blink.

"Oh, look," Myrindi continued. "I think I hit a nerve."

Lep looked to his wife for a quick update. "Chas?"

The demon's green eyes rolled back into her head for a few seconds and then snapped forward once more. "All clear."

"Thanks, honey bunches." Lep stood, groaning as his knees cracked, and then shuffled a few steps toward Myrindi and Froman. "Here's the deal: we're being paid an awful lot of money to get you out of Talvayne by someone who knew the hit on your father was coming."

Myrindi shifted uncomfortably. "Who?"

Lep scratched the back of his head, clearly embarrassed. "We don't know."

"Lovely. So what...you're for sale to the highest bidder, consequences be damned?"

"Only if the amount of money is really, really big."

"Is it?"

"Oh yeah."

"It's flattering to know I'm worth a small mint to some scumbag out there, but your impending riches don't really help me answer the whole trust question I inquired about earlier."

Pike suddenly spoke up. He almost sounded nervous. "I know who hired us."

Lep spun around and glowered at his friend. "No, you fucking don't! We've been over this. You just have a complex."

"What sort of complex?" Myrindi asked, hungry for any dirt she could hang over the elven asshole's head.

"He's in loooooooo-ooooooooooooooove," Chas teased.

Pike ignored her. "We were hired by a woman named Rayn. This is just the sort of shit she would pull."

"Axzar's taint, Pikey, the Witch isn't fucking behind fucking everything!" Lep snapped. They'd clearly had this argument before. "You fart and you think the Witch gave you gas. You wake up too late and you think she hexed your alarm clock. You—"

"Actually," Myrindi interjected, "this is exactly the type of shit she would pull."

Everyone else in the room froze, their attention glued to the princess. Pike's jaw dropped. Froman looked up at her expectantly like an annoyed parent waiting for an explanation about the turd on the kitchen floor.

"We're besties," she offered, punctuating that sentence with an emphatic ending that declared she wasn't in the mood to get into it deeper. "Although I personally think her taste in mercenaries could use some serious improvement, I'll roll with it for now. So! How are we getting out of Talvayne?"

"One step at a time, sweetheart," Lep replied. "We'll wait here til nightfall, then we'll leave the palace and take refuge elsewhere. We'll hide out tomorrow, then relocate the following night. Lather, rinse, repeat until we cross the Rot into the surrounding jungle."

"Why can't we use the transpoint network and just teleport somewhere nice and warm and far away?" Myrindi asked.

"Sorrin's already disconnected the main transpoints servicing the city," Chastity explained. "And the bootleg pair we used to reach Talvayne in the first place self-destructed."

"Also the sort of shit Rayn would pull," Pike growled.

"I want out of this shithole *now*," the princess snapped. "And I still need to tinkle."

"It's a big city, Princess," Froman said soothingly. "Moving cautiously is a wise plan, especially with the transpoints down. We don't know how many others Sorrin's brought to his side or who they might be."

"Bunch of douchebags, that's who." And then she remembered that all of the men who'd been with Sorrin when he'd killed her father were trolls of the Royal Guard. "No offense, Fro."

"None taken. I agree with your assessment."

"Great," Lep said sarcastically. "I'm glad that's settled. Know anything about Sorrin or his forces that might help us?"

"He's a giant skid mark on the underpants of life," Myrindi replied. "He's pitching a hissy fit because he was supposed to marry me but then my father found a better deal."

"He's a wood nymph," Froman added. "Served as ambassador to Evitankari and a few small ex-pat settlements."

"So he could have outside connections helping him. Wonderful. What about the trolls?"

"Who knows what goes on in their knobby little pea-brains," Myrindi muttered. "No offense, Fro."

Froman had long ago become immune to his charge's inadvertent insults and thus paid her no mind. "I'm not sure why so many of my kind cast their lot with the usurper. Our young often feel disenfranchised by their relative lack of representation in the Conclave of Kings. It's possible Sorrin is preying upon those sentiments. The Captain of the Guard—Gaptorix—was among them, which does not bode well."

"So we're flying blind," Lep replied, clearly perturbed.

"We'll be able to run recon once we're in the city proper," Chas said. "Get the lay of the land, all that. Someone's bound to know something. Regicide isn't the sort of crime that happens in a vacuum."

"Good point, sugar booger. The three of us likely haven't been identified yet. Pretty sure we didn't leave any of the trolls guarding the princess's chambers alive. Everybody get some rest and make sure you're ready to move by nightfall. If that means peeing in a damn bucket, then you'd better sack up and pee in a damn bucket. Getting out of this place ain't gonna be easy."

Lep returned to the poker game, lowered his heavy girth back down to the cement floor, and tossed a few more chips into the pot. Pike didn't notice. He continued to stare at Myrindi, as he had since she'd admitted her acquaintance with Rayn, until the princess finally got sick of it a few seconds later and flipped him off. He returned the gesture and doubled Lep's bet in annoyance.

"Princess," Fro whispered hesitantly, "what do you know of this Rayn character?"

"I told you: we're besties."

Dear Diary,

I'm sure you're as anxious to learn about my association with Rayn as Fro and that mouth-breathing lout in the tacky red armor, but we'll get to that. Trust me when I say it'll be easier to get a handle on me and my BFF if I fill you in on what went down with Sorrin, my first fiancé.

Lard Ass decided to introduce me to my betrothed while also taking me to see the Rot for the first time. You might think this is the point where I accuse my father of actually having a sense of humor, but you'd be sorely mistaken. Lard Ass doesn't—well, didn't, but forgive me for struggling with tense in his case because becoming an orphan is a major adjustment—have an ironic bone in his body. Or if he did, it was buried so deeply in his overflowing cellulite that it long ago suffocated to death. His vocabulary left a little to be desired, too, even though he knew eighty different synonyms for the word "dessert." To Lard Ass, irony was that part of his laundry the help could never get quite right.

I was ten years old at the time, and suffice to say I was not even remotely happy about being forced to rearrange my jam-packed schedule to satisfy my father's stupid whims. It got me out of my two o'clock playdate with that walking, talking fashion faux pas named Nella, though, so I made do. It only hailed briefly in downtown Talvayne.

Rarely have I had such difficulty identifying an appropriate outfit. The area afflicted with the Rot is a solemn, somber place spoken of in hushed tones when it's spoken of at all. Unless I'm talking about it; then it's probably being spoken of at an inappropriate volume that makes everyone uncomfortable. Whatever. Anyway, black seemed like the proper choice for mourning those we lost to the long-ago environmental apoca-lypse, but such dour tones could be interpreted as a signal that the crown's repeated promises to rehabilitate the affected area is, as I've long suspected, just a bunch of hot air designed to put a shiny glow on a hopeless situation. I mean, if generations of our greatest sorcerers couldn't undo the damage, why should we expect some new schmucks to get it right? I settled on a dark purple dress I didn't particularly like and wouldn't mind seeing ruined. The Rot, after all, sounded a bit dirty. No need to sacrifice something nice just to visit a dump, right?

Fro escorted me to meet my father and his entourage outside of the stables at eleven sharp that morning. As usual, Lard Ass was surrounded by a dozen guards—all trolls—and a motley collection of sycophants stumbling all over each other to plant their lips upon his ample behind. All of the men were part of the Conclave of Kings, which only made their boot-licking all the more insipid. They'd been in my father's position before; they should've known how to play the game a little bit better.

Oh, about that Conclave: it's a legislative body made up of former Kings of Talvayne. When the Crown Princess marries, her father concedes the throne to her husband and joins his predecessors in a sort of cabinet that manages various parts of our government. They also run the city when the king is unable to do so, and they can veto any of his decisions via unanimous vote, which has happened maybe twice in the Conclave's history. The active king can almost always find some turd in the punchbowl willing to throw his vote in exchange for an appropriate bribe. Usually the Conclave has about two dozen members at a time, depending on the lifespans of the species involved.

I recognized most of the kings from previous functions. There was Shit-for-Brains, a tall, lean gnoll with a horse face full of teeth that would've reduced my orthodontist to a blubbering mess. Piss Yellow and Hooker Red flittered around each other as usual; the two pixies never went anywhere without each other. Litter Box, a sand nymph, leaned against the stable wall with a lit menthol dangling from his grainy lips, doing his damnedest to look too cool for school and failing miserably. And then there was Twat Face, a scrawny little wood nymph who leered at everybody as if he were about to invite them back to his panel van to show them a puppy.

What? I said I recognized them. I didn't say I knew their real fucking names. A Talvayan Crown Princess has plenty on her plate without also having to learn the names of every minor bureaucrat trying to suck her father's fat blue dick—even though the kings were technically family. Grandfathers. Yeah, it's weird, and it doesn't translate into nearly as many birthday presents as you might think. Suffice to say we ain't close. None of them's ever made an effort. Not that I'd react positively if one did.

There were a few others, none of whom merited a nickname, and of course each was attended by his own small group of assistants or family members. Litter Box had brought his mistress, a bluish will-o-the-wisp. I'm not sure how that one worked physically, to be honest. Twat Face's adult son stood at his side, looking even scrawnier and more useless than his old man. The entire crew—well, those capable of wearing clothing, of course—was dressed in khaki uniforms and pith helmets as if they were about to explore the deepest, darkest reaches of Africa. I was glad to have missed the memo about coordinating our outfits. A family of four could've used Lard Ass's inappropriately short shorts as a sleeping bag. The deepest, darkest thing he's ever explored is a chocolate lava cake.

When Fro and I arrived, my father was making his usual show of inspecting his carriage. I've always hated that thing. Drawn forth by a pair of unicorns named Stardust and Twinkles, it's basically a huge white pumpkin on four spindly wagon wheels. Supposedly an elf in Evitankari grew it in his backyard, carriage-ified it, and presented the resulting piece of junk to a previous king a few hundred years ago. It's been the official Royal Conveyance ever since. I would've sent it back and demanded a Ferrari instead. Yes, I'm a magical princess, but that doesn't mean I want to ride around in something that looks like it got shat out by an off-brand children's cartoon. It's stuffy, it shakes like a gnome on speed, and its unnecessarily hard seats offer piss-poor lumbar support. If Cinderella had pulled up to the ball in that thing, the bouncer behind the velvet rope would've laughed at her and suggested she try the farmer's market up the street instead.

"What a fine piece of magical engineering!" my father crowed as he rubbed the abomination's smooth outer wall, making his way toward the unicorns. Gaptorix, his captain of the guard, hovered over him like a mother hen with a ridiculous steroid regimen and a history as a cage fighter.

"Still in tip-top shape, Your Highness!" Twat Face said.

"Not another like it in the world!" Litter Box added.

"Good," I whispered to Fro. "Then we won't be able to get a new one when I light it on fire."

As usual, Twinkles whinnied and pawed the ground excitedly as my father patted his glittering white flank. Also as usual, Stardust gave my father the stink eye and took a rainbow-colored dump on the cobblestones. I liked Stardust better.

"We're off to the edge of the Rot today, fellas," Lard Ass said as he stroked Twinkles's sleek white mane. Unicorns will go wherever they're told without requiring a driver to navigate or keep them in line. Science has proven them to be lazy creatures who hate thinking for themselves—kind of like male pop stars or television news anchors. "Head north by northeast, between Par's Gorge and the Great Foam." He turned to me. "But first, there's someone I'd like to introduce to you."

I rolled my eyes and sighed. "Who?"

"This young man's name is Sorrin," he replied, indicating Twat Face Jr. "When you're sixteen, you'll marry him."

That set off a series of alarms in my head. Frowning, I studied Sorrin closely. All wood nymphs are spindly little things that resemble old-timey puppets, but Sorrin is especially frail. His wooden skin is the color of polished oak. Little green leaves sprout from his body wherever he should have hair. Unfortunately, he inherited most of his father's face. I'd known since before birth that my destiny was to grow up, marry the new king, and bear an heir of his species, but somehow I'd always pictured my future husband as a more regal individual. Sorrin looked like something a child would toss in a toy box and forget about.

"Pleased to make your acquaintance, Myrindi," he said with a polite nod of his head.

Scowling, I looked up at my father. "Really? That nancy's going to be king?"

Every jaw on every male around me dropped. I swear I could feel the testosterone being sucked out of that courtyard. Stardust whinnied merrily.

Lard Ass shifted his girth and planted his hands on his ample hips in a vain impression of authority. "We'll discuss this after the day's events, young lady."

"Works for me." Dealing with a surprise fiancee was not something for which I was prepared.

Only five of us would be riding inside the Royal Conveyance. It could've fit eight, but...well, you know, Lard Ass. Three of my father's troll guards got down on their hands and knees to form a staircase. We clambered atop them and up inside. I was wedged between Fro and my father's thigh fat just beside one of the carriage's two tiny windows. Twat Face and his son took the two remaining seats. The remainder of the party either hoofed it or rode in smaller, less obnoxious carts drawn by normal old horses.

One of the guards shut the door and the unicorns started forward. Lard Ass and Twat Face began a heated discussion about the legality of live poultry use in geomancy or some stupid shit I didn't care about. Fro, as he tended to do, closed his eyes to meditate. That left me with no one to talk to but Twat Face's son, and I really, really didn't like the possessive way that jerk was looking at me. Turning in my seat, I leaned back against my father's shoulder, draped my legs across Fro's, and turned my attention to the scene outside the carriage's little window. I did so just in time to catch our passage through the Gate of Illumination, the Palace of Light's primary entrance and exit. From the outside, it looked like any other castle gate: a solid, sturdy trio of closed portcullises surrounded by heavy gray stone. The view from inside, however, was much different. The portcullises didn't exist, and the cobblestones inside glowed an eerie yellow color. Passing through the Gate of Illumination was like walking through a prism. Every color in the spectrum bounced around the stone interior like some sort of laser show on crack. I've spent many fruitless years attempting to find a tailor who could reproduce the effect in a formal gown. A girl can dream, can't she?

I've always been fascinated with Talvayne proper. Our city is a mish-mash of twisting streets, clashing landscapes, and random architecture that would give an urban planner an immediate stroke. The diverse collection of races that calls Talvayne home makes some semblance of sense when viewed as a unit—specifically, one called "not human"—but when you break it all down into its component parts, it's easy to wonder just what the hell everybody's thinking. My people, for instance, like things to be a bit wet. Twat Face and his ilk live in densely wooded areas, and I trust you're smart enough to figure out what sort of environment Litter Box, the sand nymph, prefers. Luckily for everybody involved, Talvayne's land is super responsive to its citizens; thanks to the magic of the king, it adjusts itself to fit whoever lives upon it. It's normal to find a stand of hundred-foot redwoods abutting a shimmering ocean, a soaring mountain pocked with caves, a series of dunes awash with a roiling sandstorm, and a frigid iceberg. The narrow cobblestone streets just sort of adjust themselves on the fly as needed. Even the Palace of Light modifies its internal temperature and humidity to adjust for the species of the Royal Family. Sure, it all seems unnecessarily complicated and it would make a lot more sense, say, to have just one big desert, one big forest, and so on and so forth, but it all just sort of works on its own as long as there's a king so no one's ever really messed with it. Way to go, Talvayne. Best customer service ever. So much better than the cable company, am I right?

Anyway, that constantly shifting view makes a ride in Father's stupid carriage almost tolerable. Imagine how enjoyable it would be in a hot pink convertible, top down, your favorite dance mix blasting from the stereo. Of course, when you're a Talvayan Crown Princess, you really aren't allowed to have that much fun, regardless of how many thunderstorms you cause while pleading your case. There's only one of me, after all, and I really can't be risked. Still, the palace gets a little boring at times, you know?

Turns out men who buy wives can't handle being ignored. Twat Face Jr. leaned across the carriage and tapped me on the knee. I recoiled in revulsion. "Don't touch me."

"My apologies, Your Highness, but I feel it important to clear the air between us and establish my bona fides. I'm not the useless little rich boy you believe me to be. I spent sixteen years as my father's primary adviser during his reign as king and another forty in foreign relations, working primarily with the elves of Evitankari to assure continued cooperation between our great nations."

"Good for you."

Sorrin's smile grew even wider. "If you prefer deeds to words, Princess, then I'll just have to do my best to sweep you off your feet and prove my worth."

"You do that," I said, rolling my eyes. I turned back to my father. "Clooney's available. I'll have the servants get his number."

"Girl's got high standards," Twat Face Jr. said merrily. "But I assure you all I'm up to the challenge."

"Up to the challenge? Do I *look* like a crossword puzzle or a cheesy reality TV show obstacle course? I'm a Talvayan Crown

Princess, buster, and you ain't fit to lick my ass sweat off the Throne of Light."

"Myrindi!" Lard Ass snapped. "What did I tell you about respecting people who deserve it?"

"You told me to respect people who deserve it," I replied, confused. "I fail to see how that applies to this situation."

"Don't worry about the Princess, Your Highness," Sorrin interjected calmly. "I imagine this all comes as a sudden shock to her. I'm sure once she's spent more time with me our love will blossom like a beautiful flower in the Glittering Gardens."

"More like a fart in the wind," I muttered. Beside me, Fro barely suppressed a snort.

The conversation shifted back to banal government machinations and—even worse—flareball, the supposed national pastime of Talvayne. Why so many supposedly grown-ass men want to watch a bunch of wisps ping-pong around the inside of a giant bathtub is beyond me. I redirected my attention to the window and watched the scenery roll past as I considered this latest forced redirection of my life plan. I've always pictured myself shacking up with someone dashing and worldly, a gentleman and a scholar as handsome as he is well-spoken and fashionable. Perhaps he'd spent some time studying mysticism among a hidden cabal of mute monks or taken a semester off from college to paint seascapes in the Philippines. Regardless, he hadn't let his experiences go to his head, and he exuded a certain down-to-earth realism that mixed with his brash confidence to make my heart melt and my woo-woo quiver.

I glanced clandestinely at Sorrin. Twat Face Jr. most certainly did not fit that description. He'd be great as a used car salesman, I thought, or perhaps as the annoying roommate in a direct-to-video romcom, but he totally wasn't cut out to be either king or *my* husband. I only get one, after all, and there isn't a divorce lawyer in the world who'd have the balls to take my case.

Plus—well, you know, there's that whole dying-via-child-birth-to-transfer-anti-Rot-magic-to-the-new-princess thing Talvayan queens are all required to do. People know—I mean, how could they not—but it's a touchy subject never brought up in the sort of polite conversation that typically surrounds princesses. I've never asked anyone about it because that would be a bit morbid. Anyway, back to my point. If I'm going to die a painful death nine months after my husband knocks me up, I'd prefer to die a painful death for someone who's worth it, not some ugly little twit who got the gig because his father gave my father a herd of goats and some gift certificates to the local ice cream parlor. Arranged marriages suck.

Outside, a volcano's smoking crater gave way to a green field of hearty grass tall enough to swallow ten-year-old me. My mind whirled a mile a minute. Twat Face Jr. had to go, of course, but what would be the best way to get rid of him? I knew from my mother that such deals weren't immediately etched in stone, that they weren't considered truly final until the day of the princess's wedding. Technically that meant I'd have six years to figure it all out—as Lard Ass mentioned, we marry on our sixteenth birthdays—but I wanted to be rid of this loser as quickly as possible. Mother had spent years attending various functions with my father before her own wedding, and I really didn't want to spend any more time with Sorrin than was absolutely necessary.

My options seemed few and far between. If I could find someone to outbid the Twat Face family, Sorrin's father would still have the opportunity to present a counter-proposal, and the last thing I wanted to do was trigger a bidding war that would make Lard Ass even richer. Perhaps, I thought, our destination that day would prove convenient. The Rot was a dangerous place few dared tread without royal protection. A little "accident" could be just what I needed.

As we moved further out of the city, the plots of land we passed became smaller and less stable, often seeping into each other in oddly captivating forms that wouldn't have been possible anywhere else. Ever seen a desert oasis surrounded by a glacier or a green forest pocked with patches of ocean? Trust me, it's messed up, like a Versace gown some single mom from the 'burbs covered with homemade rhinestones. You want to look away, but you just can't. Out there, far from the palace, the king's magic isn't strong enough to force the land to make some damn sense. Maybe things would've been better if my father tried harder, but no one calling that particular neighborhood home would've been able to make a realistic bid for his daughter's hand in marriage, if you catch my drift. Wrong side of the metaphorical tracks.

After a four-and-half-hour ride, the carriage stopped beside a plot of arctic tundra trimmed with palm trees and the sort of red stone arch you only see in pictures of the desert transformed into desktop wallpaper. "We're here!" my father declared as if he were announcing the Oscar winner for Best Picture. Lard Ass's basic observational skills are...well, were... always top notch.

The door puckered open and three troll guards once again knelt beside the carriage to form a staircase. Fro disembarked first to check the scene for possible threats, as he always did whenever I traveled farther than my own private washroom. I would've preferred he not turn his back on the Twat Face family, but maybe he thought I could take the scrawny little stick men on my own if I had to. The two wood nymphs exited next. It would've been pretty impossible for Lard Ass to squeeze around them.

"After you," my father said, motioning me forward.

I wrinkled my pretty little nose. "It smells like feet out there."

"Of course it does. That's the Rot."

"So you're saying that Axzar jerk cursed Talvayne with a giant ring of rancid athlete's foot?"

Lard Ass's face darkened. "It is very unbecoming of a princess to speak that way about the greatest wound ever inflicted upon her culture."

I probably would've classified that stupid carriage as such instead, but I let the matter slide. "I'm not going to catch anything by just breathing it in, am I?"

He shook his head. "The Rot spreads via contact only, and besides: all Talvayan princesses are born immune. It's the magic within you, passed on to you via the love of your mother, that holds the Rot at bay and protects our great city from its vile hunger."

I knew all this, of course. Every tutor I'd learned under had insisted on drilling it into my head. For some reason Lard Ass always liked telling me things I was already aware of. If he ever comes back as a ghost, the first thing he'll probably say to me is "Myrindi, I'm dead." Thanks, Pops. Thanks a lot.

It smelled even worse outside of the carriage, and the Rot looked just like something that emits that sort of stench should look. A black and brown stain covered the land before us. Rather than destroying what it touched, the Rot held its victims frozen in time, covering trees, vegetation, and people alike, turning the area around Talvayne into a sort of still-life-in-shit that never changed. Where it abutted healthy land the Rot was more fluid than it was solid, rolling in gentle waves that lapped hungrily at the soil it couldn't take. It was really fucking gross.

"Axzar wanted to do something to us we would never, ever forget," Froman whispered, nodding toward a humanoid figure caked in the stuff, frozen forever in a mad run toward safety. "I'd say he succeeded."

About a hundred or so Talvayan residents had gathered for the occasion. The Royal Family rarely leaves the palace together, so our trip out to the Rot was kind of a big deal. Beside me, Father lurched into the sort of melodramatic, blustery speech he seemed required by law to make everywhere he went. I was too busy giving the Rot the stink eye to really care. Coming face-to-taint with the reason my mother had died so young pissed me off in a way that had never happened before and hadn't happened again until I met Pike. In the distance, thunder rumbled. "This is stupid," I snarled.

Around me, everyone gasped. Lard Ass stopped spewing garbage to look down at me like I'd just told him dinner was going to be a salad. "I beg your pardon," he rumbled, his rolls quivering in annoyance. "This is a sacred area where—"

"We live in the middle of a giant skid mark," I snapped. The thunder rumbled again, closer this time, and dark, puffy clouds slowly gathered in the sky. "Why?"

"Because, in an effort to stop our mighty army from rallying to Evitankari's side, Axzar unleashed a curse—"

"Yeah, yeah, I know that part. It's in all the history books. That's not my question. I want to know why we're going to all the trouble of living in a place that would be swallowed by predatory slime mold if not for some pretty powerful magic."

Lard Ass just stared at me, obviously at a complete loss for words. Sorrin stepped around him and offered an answer. "Talvayne is our home," he said gently. "Why should we leave it, Your Highness?"

"Because packing our bags and hitting the road probably would've been a hell of a lot easier and more humane than whipping up a ridiculous magic spell passed on to future generations via death in the birthing room."

Nobody spoke. Nobody moved.

I rolled my eyes and balled my fists. "Ugh, you are all so dense!" I growled. Wind began whipping and howling all around us, leaving the kings and their guests glancing warily at the darkening sky. Turning, I took a step toward the Rot, intending to give it a serious piece of my mind. It flinched away at my approach, hissing like a startled cobra, which in turn stopped me in my tracks because I'd never seen or heard an ocean of shit do that before.

"Ah, so you're afraid of me, is that it?" I asked the Rot. It didn't answer. I took another step and it recoiled even further. The small, round swath of land it exposed was cracked and dry and dead. Struck by a tremendously brilliant idea, I continued forward toward the edge. The Rot responded by pulling back again, offering me a short, narrow path into its midst as it struggled to keep its distance. I took it.

"Myrindi, stop!" Lard Ass bellowed. "Come away from there, child!"

But I kept going. The clear path continued to adjust itself around me as the Rot fled my presence. A few steps deeper and it shifted to fill the gap behind me, just as I'd hoped. I wasn't afraid; if I'd been in any real danger, Fro never would've let me get so close. I ignored the panicked shouts of my father and his guests and pressed on.

When I finally turned, there was about fifteen feet of Rot between me and the others. Lard Ass and the kings eyed the edge anxiously and begged me to come back. Fro leaned against the carriage, watching with what I could've sworn was amusement. A distressed murmur burbled up from the cluster of citizens in attendance.

The sky above cleared, turning the brightest blue I'd ever seen. I closed my eyes and raised my face into the sunlight's warm embrace. I'd been a thorn in my father's side for years, but this was the first time I felt like I'd ever really put one over on him. I could've walked through the Rot forever and he wouldn't have been able to stop me. That, really, was what Lard Ass and the kings were so worried about: I'd put myself out of their reach and there was nothing they could do about it.

But it smelled really bad out there, so I decided to get to the point. "Oh!" I shrieked, pretending to swoon. "I'm stuck out in the Rot! Won't one of you big, strong men come save me?"

If I'd been able to take a picture of the looks on their faces I would've blown it up and hung it above my bed. Lard Ass and the kings stared at me like I'd lit myself on fire. They probably wished I had; it would've been better than making them look impotent in front of a crowd that was getting bigger by the second. For generations the Talvayan Crown Princess had always been their personal property, an asset they could trade back and forth between each other as part of the stupid political games they were all addicted to. I'd just given them a dose of their own medicine, and they had no clue how to handle it. Mother would've been so proud.

And she would've given me the most enthusiastic high-five ever for what I did next. "Oh! Sorrin!" I howled. "Won't the man who will be my king save me from this horrible predicament?"

Twat Face Jr. gaped at me. I swear I heard his tiny wooden balls fall off and land on the ground.

"Do something!" a female voice cried out from the crowd. "That's our princess out there!"

That one citizen opened up the floodgate that had been holding back the others. The crowd rained insults and challenges down upon the kings, entreating them to do something, anything, to save their princess—and making it clear that if they didn't, well, they were a bunch of good-for-nothing bureaucrats who didn't deserve their riches or their stations. Which was the truth, really, but judging from the looks on the kings' faces they weren't used to being reminded of that fact so bluntly. The half dozen or so troll guards who'd accompanied our party shifted their attention from the scene in the Rot to the abusive group of citizens that now had them all surrounded.

"Save our princess, you twits!" a large gnoll shouted.

"You're all so fucking useless!" a female sand nymph screamed. "How'd you let her get out there in the first place!"

"*That's* our next king?" a tiny old gnome asked incredulously. "If he can't help her, he has no right!"

To be honest, the crowd's response came as a complete surprise to me. My tutors had always insisted that the citizenry loved and adored the king and the Conclave as heroes beyond reproach who never did anything wrong—you know, like Kim and Kourtney. I'd always thought I was the only one who really knew they were just a bunch of bumbling clowns with inflated egos. Granted, I'd learned that from Mother, but still. It was nice to have some backup for once, you know?

And I didn't like the way Father's guards were looking at that backup. Sure, they were a bunch of poor, dirty peasants who likely contributed at least a little to the area's peculiar odor, but they were on *my side*. I'd had my fun and made my point and it was time to defuse the situation I'd caused, even though I kind of wished I could've stayed out there forever. I bet the Rot would've made more room for a sofa and a television if I'd asked it nicely. I took one tentative step back toward Talvayne, feigning fear even though I knew the roiling shit on the ground wanted to touch me about as much as I wanted to touch Sorrin on our future wedding night.

"I think...I think it's okay, everybody!" I shouted, letting my voice quiver just a little for added I'm-afraid-but-look-how-brave-I-am effect. "I think I can make it! This stuff is sooooooooo gross!"

The crowd's angry heckling shifted into a shower of support as I exited the Rot the same way I'd entered. With each step I allowed a little bit more of my confidence to show. My slow, tentative shuffling steadily grew into an arrogant, hip-shaking swagger. Not that I really had much in the way of hips, but I worked it as hard as I could. I gave my new fans a coy wave of appreciation as I crossed the final few feet back onto healthy land, making sure they knew I was grateful for their contributions. They'd given my little show a better finale than I ever could've hoped for.

My father's eyes were dead. "We're going home," he grumbled.

— CHAPTER FOUR —

C hastity sighed. "They're coming."
A tiny spark burst to life in the top left-hand corner of the door, crackling and popping like the end of a lit fuse. It slowly traced its way downward as if someone were cutting through with some sort of torch or laser.

"Actually, looks like they're here," Myrindi said.

"Can you slow them down?" Lep whispered. Pike, noticing his friend's momentary distraction, scraped up the bills in the current poker game's pot and shoved them into his pocket.

"Sure thing, hon, but if I do that they'll know for sure we're in here *and* we'll give them time to call reinforcements."

"So don't slow it down," the princess suggested. "Speed it up and surprise the bastards."

Lep and Pike traded confused glances. "That's...actually kind of brilliant," Chastity said.

"And very, very dangerous," Froman added. "That strategy will put the princess in a lot of danger."

Lep nodded his agreement. "There isn't a lot of room to maneuver in here. We'll have to burst out into the hallway and take the fight to them."

The old troll wasn't convinced. "And if we're overcome or flanked, then what?" He stood, scanning the room with his beady little eyes. His attention settled on a tiny rusted grate in the floor near the far back corner. "Princess, that's your way out. Leave the fighting to us."

Myrindi wrinkled her nose. "Talvayan Crown Princesses do *not* travel through heating ducts."

"She's right," Pike growled. "Talvayan Crown Princesses only travel in hot pink bitchmobiles."

Froman stepped between the two before things could escalate. He put his rough, gnarled hands on the princess's smooth shoulders. "Your Highness, I ask that you trust me. The four of us will stand a better chance against whatever's out there if we aren't concerned with your immediate safety."

Understanding dawned briefly in the princess's eyes, but she immediately hid it under her usual temper. "It's dirty down there. And I bet there's spiders."

"Spiders are not a thing Talvayan Crown Princesses need fear, my dear." The troll's rough voice rose an octave and became surprisingly gentle and understanding. "Plus...a left turn to the next vent should drop you down a floor and right into the ladies' room attached to the archives."

Myrindi thrust her journal into Froman's chest. The troll took it in both hands as if she'd just handed him her child. "You're right, of course," the princess said as she strode over to stand above the grate. "I'll be in the washroom. Find me when you're done with the rabble outside, but please don't dispatch them so quickly that I don't have time to tinkle."

"Yes, ma'am," Pike grumbled. "We'll be sure to kill them slowly for the glory of the Royal Bladder."

"On behalf of the Royal Bladder: thanks, asshole!" Myrindi snapped. "Turn around, all of you. This is a lot easier in the buff."

"Last thing I want to see," Pike muttered as he turned around and looked at the floor. Lep and Froman did the same, but Chastity just covered her eyes with her hands.

Myrindi shucked her dress and her underwear, closed her eyes, and took a deep breath. Her flesh shifted suddenly into water, then collapsed down through the grate and into the palace's heating system.

Dear Diary,

I don't know if you can hear me or not, but I'm going to pretend you can because it'll give me something to focus on while I navigate this gross fucking duct. Being able to turn into a mobile, sentient puddle sounds really cool until you actually do it. The transition feels really funny, almost like every part of your body is tinkling at once. Yeah, I still have to go and I can't quite get it out of my mind. Sue me. But it's not just the change that's annoying. Moving is really, really hard unless there's other water to slip into that's going in the general direction you're aiming for. No water? Hope you're ready for a struggle. I'd be sweating like a gnoll right now if I still had glands. Ever tried to make a puddle move uphill? Right. Of course you haven't. You're just a book. Just trust me when I say it's about as much fun as trying to teach Pike his multiplication tables. Or trying to teach Pike how to use the TV remote. Or trying to teach Pike to walk and chew gum at the same time. I'm sure you get the picture.

Anyway. Back to my exciting escapades with Twat Face Jr. The dramatic scene I caused in the Rot put a major hurt on the little stump's reputation, but he took it as a challenge of sorts. Sorrin's a goof, but you can't question his perseverance. He came to visit me about a week later. Gaptorix accompanied him to the doors of my chambers and announced his arrival in just the booming baritone you'd expect from such a walking, talking battleship. "Ambassador Sorrin, Royal Ambassador to Evitankari and Other Places Magical, to see Myrindi, Crown Princess of Talvayne!" he roared. It was more like his mouth was a cannon bombarding an enemy harbor.

I ignored him for a few moments and idly flipped to the next page in the issue of *Cosmo* I was reading on my favorite sofa, a super modern deal trimmed in red velvet that perfectly matched the curtains of my parlor's four towering windows while also going well with the dark hardwood floor. I had just finished reading the third entry in a Five Best Looks for Fall article and I wasn't about to delay numbers four and five to hang out with Twat Face Jr. Pro tip, girls: fashion should *always* take priority over unwanted romantic advances, doubly so when said advances are due to an arranged marriage in which you had zero input.

Ten minutes passed. I'd finished the article but felt the need to review it. *Cosmo*, after all, is famous for the sort of nuanced writing that often requires multiple readings to properly digest. I hope the work I'm laying down on your pages, Diary, is at least half as good. But yeah, I totally left Sorrin and Gaptorix hanging. So what? It's not like either of them had possessed the foresight to register a proper appointment with my chief-of-staff. Sorrin should've been disqualified from any and all kingly opportunities solely for his inability to schedule a simple meeting.

Five more minutes later, Twat Face Jr. decided he could stroll right into my private suite without being invited. He sauntered across the marble threshold like he owned the joint, decked out in a crisp white toga with golden thread that couldn't have been more last summer. In his left hand he carried a bouquet of yellow and purple roses that glittered in the midday light streaming in through the windows. A smarmy smile stretched his wooden face wide so he looked like some sort of pornographic jack-o-lantern. Skeeziness radiated off his bark like heat off the ground on a sweltering day. Sorrin had decided to go a-courtin', and he was going all out to nail his target.

"Fuck me," I mumbled under my breath, wrinkling my nose at the stench of his pungent cologne. I glanced anxiously to the far corner where Fro sat meditating atop a big white pillow. Simple breaches of etiquette, unfortunately, did not fall under his jurisdiction. He'd opened one eye as soon as Gaptorix arrived, however, and he was ready and waiting to step in should my safety come into question. Even bad-ass bodyguards have to follow the rules.

"Ah, Princess!" Sorrin chirped as he stepped onto the white shag carpet I'd installed around my sitting area. "You look positively ravishing this afternoon!"

Sensing that he wouldn't go away if I just continued staring at my magazine, I looked up and fixed him with a glare that would've stripped the paint off a sports car. "You look like you just stepped out of an old pizza commercial."

His smile somehow got even bigger. "Ah, always the clever one! I do so look forward to your verbal acrobatics. I'm sure similar banter will fill our marriage with whimsy and laughter."

The bastard was up to something. In spite of myself, I kind of wanted to know what. Keep your enemies close, right? "What, pray tell, is so important that you thought it pertinent to barge straight into my private chambers without an invitation? It had better be good, or I will personally see to it that your reputation is thoroughly destroyed within all of Talvayne's highest social circles."

Twat Face Jr. feigned contrition. "Is wishing to spend time with one's betrothed such a crime?"

"I've petitioned my father to incorporate a law against that very thing. He's working on it."

The wood nymph sat down beside me on the sofa, again without being invited. I couldn't tell if he was brave or just stupid. From his cushion in the corner, Fro cleared his throat loudly to make sure Sorrin knew he was there. The wood nymph didn't care. "Your Highness, let me assure you it would be a sad day indeed if your father put an end to such a thing. Surely one as wise and worldly as yourself understands the joys of love."

I blinked at him in annoyance. "I'm ten."

He offered me the bouquet he'd brought along. It smelled like a troll's asshole. Sorry, Fro, but you get a little ripe after Taco Tuesday. Why did you think I always insisted the maids open all the windows afterward? It wasn't because I fart. I'm a princess. I don't pass gas.

"Luckily, Your Highness, you've got a fiancé to help you with that."

"I can think of something I could use your help with."

He perked up at that. "Anything, my darling."

"Get those weeds out of my face. Next time, spend the extra money on the flitteroses. They're worth the few bucks extra." Truth is, the price difference was much larger. Twat Face Jr. was just a good-for-nothing cheapskate. He probably bought that shitty bouquet with a coupon.

Undeterred, he set the flowers down on the opposite side of the sofa. "Noted. When we're married, our chambers will be full of beautiful flitteroses."

"That won't be necessary," I replied. "We'll be living in separate suites. First thing we're going to do is teach you how power couples really work: smiles and chaste smooches in public, no reason to talk or even look at each other in private. You're more than welcome to take on a mistress or two."

Twat Face Jr. laughed heartily. I considered punching him in the balls but thought better of it. "Princess, your sense of humor never ceases to astound me. Where do you come up with such things? There's a brilliant mind inside Your Highness's pretty little head. Brains and beauty; I couldn't be luckier! All jokes aside, however, our marriage will be one built upon a solid foundation of love and respect."

"Our marriage will be based on the fact that your father had something my father wanted," I growled. "It'll be a business arrangement, nothing more."

Sorrin's smile flipped upside down into the sort of melodramatically oppressed frown that had been out of style since the vaudeville days. "I can't deny it's business that's brought us together, Your Highness. Our fathers are just doing what they know best: making a transaction. But by no means are the two of us required to treat our relationship the same way. Love often blossoms in the strangest of places under less than ideal circumstances." He paused to pat the cushion between my foot and his knee. "I believe love can grow right here, between us."

Here's the thing about Sorrin: he usually gets a lot of the words right. I'm sure you're thinking I'm a bitch and I'm going to drop some of my patented verbal ninjitsu on his ass even though he's trying to make the best of things and doesn't deserve all the vitriol I've spat in his general direction. That's where you're wrong, Diary. Yes, Twat Face Jr.'s little speech is exactly the sort of thing a castle-bound princess with dreams of spreading her wings and exploring the larger world would want to hear from a prospective suitor. It's cheesy, yes, but it's the truth. We're suckers for that shit. Thing is, it's not what he says so much as how he says it that proves he's a disingenuous little twig. It's the little sneer twisting the corners of his mouth. It's the predatory glint in his eyes. It's the I'm-in-charge-you-peon tone that occasionally seeps into his voice when he's trying to hide his frustration. He's fooled a lot of people with his act, but he can't fool me.

And no, that's not because his act isn't all that different from my own. Don't be silly, Diary. That sort of thinking will get you thrown in the recycling bin with last month's *Vogue*. I can see through him because I'm super observant and incredibly intelligent. That's all.

"The only thing that should grow between us is distance," I replied. "And perhaps a certain chemistry of the sort enjoyed by costars on the set of a well-directed indy flick. We'll have appearances to keep up, after all."

He shifted in his seat and shook his head. "Your father told me you'd be difficult. Luckily for you, I'm not so easily deterred." He stood and straightened his toga. "Come. I've thrown you the mother of all engagement parties out in the courtyard. If words aren't enough, maybe a few deeds will be."

"Yup. Throw money at the problem. That'll help. Not like that sort of thing's the root of the issue or anything."

His wide smile oozed barely restrained anger. "If that's the way you feel, that's the way you feel. I'll be in the courtyard at our engagement party. Join me or don't. For the record, I hope you choose to attend. You only get one, after all, and it would be a shame to waste it."

I glared evilly at Twat Face Jr.'s scrawny back as he and Gaptorix left the room. He was right, just not in the way he thought. I only get one engagement party, so yeah, I might as well make the most of it. After all, you only get one chance to embarrass the shit out of your fiancé during the formal celebration of your impending nuptials. It wasn't lost on me that I'd been given zero warning about the party. Sorrin and my father were trying to keep me off balance in the hopes it would keep me in line. They didn't realize that what I'd done to them in the Rot had come completely off the cuff. Not for the first time, I wondered how much worse my life would be if my oppressors actually had a few brain cells between them.

Of course, I couldn't just follow Twat Face Jr. to the courtyard and immediately do the most annoying thing I could think of. No, no. That's not how the game is played. I lingered there on my couch for a while, turning the possibilities over in my mind and considering what to wear. The problem, of course, was the lack of an audience. My stroll into the Rot only busted so many balls because of the random citizens there to aid in the busting. If those peasants hadn't been there, the powers-that-be would've laughed it off and swept it under the rug and never spoken of it again. The bastards tend to stick together like that. Sure, there'd be more than a few servants out there in the courtyard, but I needed more than whispered rumors and scuttlebutt slowly leeching out into the city at large. I needed something big. Something dramatic. Something even Sorrin's peers couldn't excuse. But what?

I put my scheming aside and got dressed. Fashion always helps me clear my head. I definitely worked as a runway model in several past lives. This one time a couple months after all this engagement crap, my trailer trash swamp thing playmate Nella threw some *dirty* shade on my ability to play house. "The husband and wife are supposed to work together and be happy!" she said in her squeaky, annoying voice. She just couldn't get it through her head that the woman should always be in charge of the man because he's a doddering fool (it's genetic), and she became so angry with her own lack of intelligence and understanding that she flipped the plastic table on which we'd set up our tea set and stormed away. I play house like a *boss*, Diary, and I couldn't let that shit stand. So, after six hours of trying on bathing suits and floppy sun hats, I whipped up a plot that framed her father for embezzling royal funds and got her entire family kicked out of Talvayne. Problem solved.

Anyway, I didn't have the luxury of time here. After rejecting a red miniskirt, a yellow velvet pantsuit, and a maroon sheathe with a frilly neckline, I settled on a sleeveless white dress with a thin blue spiral-y thing on the left hip. Classy, but kind of dull despite that one spot of bright color. The kind of garment that looks good but says nothing at all in particular. Perfect for the company Christmas party or your least favorite cousin's baby shower. A pair of white pumps and a jangly blue bracelet completed the look. Not bad.

Fro walked me out of my chambers, down the stairs, through a short hallway, and then out to the courtyard. We didn't speak. He can be an irritating mother hen at times, but he usually knows when I don't want to be bothered. Guess that comes with the territory. You don't play personal bodyguard to eight generations of Talvayan Crown Princesses without learning a few things. He's tough to read, but I remember thinking he looked a little sad that day. Maybe he didn't approve of my engagement to Sorrin. Maybe he could tell I was up to something and just didn't want to have to deal with the consequences. Probably it was a little of both.

Whoever designed my engagement party did an amazing job. I made a mental note to have Fro get the event planner's name. Normally the courtyard is pretty boring; it's just some grass between the keep and the castle's outer wall. Nobody uses it for much. For my engagement party, a full quarter of the courtyard was transformed into an uber-modern night club. Twists of bright silvery metal sprung up out of the green grass here and there like trees, each lined with shelves of food and drink. Round tables built of a similar material offered guests places to congregate and chat. Tubes of light hovered at random intervals above it all, painting the area a gentle red. It was super pretty, but I also couldn't help thinking it was a big waste of effort.

I paused at the edge of the party and scanned the crowd. Most of those in attendance were wood nymphs like Sorrin, save for the kings and their families and a few water nymphs

I recognized as aunts and uncles. Bunch of dillholes. I waited, expecting to be announced or introduced or otherwise acknowledged. I was ignored. Probably not a surprise, huh? They weren't about to give me an invitation to cause a scene. Still, it stung a little.

"Happy engagement party to me," I muttered under my breath.

I didn't notice the tiny old wood nymph approaching until she was right on top of me. "Happy engagement party indeed," she replied, her voice creaking and cracking like a worn floor. She probably would've had an inch or two on me if she stood straight up, but her withered and crooked body was hunched badly over a gnarled wooden cane. The leaves of her hair were yellow and orange and spotted with brown. Bulky knots covered her face and hands, especially around her eyes. She wore a dress with the sort of blue floral pattern you only find at bingo night. Despite her diminutive size, her presence seemed to fill the space in front of me. Here was a woman who'd seen some shit and kicked it square in the ass.

"I don't believe I've had the pleasure," I said tentatively.

"Quansea," she croaked. "I'm the groom's great-grand-mother. I was hoping to have a few words with you."

"Of course." There wasn't much I was less interested in than getting to know the Twat Face family, but something told me the old woman wouldn't take no for answer. And it's not like anyone else was even remotely paying attention to me.

"By now I'm sure you've learned that my great-grandson is a dipshit."

I laughed. "Didn't take me long to figure that out."

"It's not a trait he's ever learned to hide. He's a lost cause, despite my best efforts. Too much like his father."

"So, what? You think I can whip him into shape? That's not really how the king-queen dynamic works around here."

It was her turn to laugh. "No, it certainly isn't, and putting him on the Throne of Light won't give the little shit any reason to grow up. He's always been a merciless, conniving bastard. What happens when he's not just above the law but made to embody it? Nothing good, I think."

"I'm with you. And I'm working on it."

Quansea nodded. "Good. I'd hate to see my great-great-granddaughter grow up the way you have. No offense."

"None taken. It sucks."

"I feel for you, dear, truly I do. None of us should be treated like possessions to be bought and sold, especially those of us who keep the city safe." She leaned forward conspiratorially. "By the way, last I saw my great-grandson, he was heading for the servants' tent with a pretty young lady who wants his money. Sorrin's never been able to control himself around an open bar."

My face flushed with anger. Did he really have the gall to mess around with someone else at our engagement party? I mean yeah, the whole thing was a sham, but the least he could've done was try to keep up appearances. "One more character flaw for the list. Which direction?"

Quansea pointed one slender finger to her left. "Give him hell."

"I'll do my worst."

"I expect nothing less."

So that was weird, right? Whole engagement party full of important people and the only one who wants to talk to the bride—who happens to be a princess, by the way—is the groom's angry great-grandmother. I kind of wish I had a relative like her, but that's just not the way this sort of thing works. Fuck you, Diary. Actually, wait...I guess technically I have a relative like her. The senior Twat Face is my great-times-X grandfather, so Quansea is my family already. And so is Sorrin. Shit. This whole thing is a mess.

Anyway. Remember that fancy red light I mentioned? It's good for more than setting the mood. It also hides all the functional parts of the event so its important guests don't have to see them. You know, because no minor dignitary or pissant former king should *ever* have to lay eyes on a pile of dirty dishes. Yes, I'm allowed to crap on snobs even though I'm a snob myself. Watch your tone, Diary. Anyway, there's a trick to seeing through the illusion: all you've got to do is close one eye. Simple, right? The spell was originally designed so the servants can dispel its effects without the use of their hands or any sort of magic words so they can carry more stuff and not sully our air with their dirty voices. It's a piece of sorcery that's become popular anywhere someone wants to hide something from anyone who doesn't know any better. I closed my left eye and the servants' tent appeared about thirty paces away from the party in the direction Quansea had indicated.

As I stomped toward the squat box of white canvas, my anger gave way to something like relief. With any luck, Sorrin had given me exactly what I was looking for: a means of legitimately hurting him. Maybe I could piss him off so badly that he'd back out of whatever deal he'd made with my father. It was my only hope, really, of ridding myself of the stupid little stump—outside of killing him, of course, which just wouldn't be very ladylike. That sort of street cred would ruin my carefully cultivated vibe of cultured sophistication.

The servants' tent was your standard issue plastic hut thing with white walls and windows that are supposed to be clear but aren't because they're covered with some sort of gross crud. I ducked under one of the ropes attaching the tent to a nearby stake and crept along beside it as quietly as I could. If I could catch Sorrin in the act, I had something that would absolutely ruin his night. The timing had to be just right, though, and I had to get close or it wouldn't work.

I rounded the next corner and almost walked right into half a dozen pixies hanging out behind the tent. The cloud of miniature winged people scattered angrily as I pulled up short. There were two men and four women, all clad in the black slacks and matching button-down shirt typical of poorly paid catering staff. All of them smoked tiny cigarettes.

A burly, bald little man with a bent left wing flittered up to my face and glared at me angrily. "Hey, watch it you—"

"Harzix!" the pale blond woman snapped. "That's the princess!"

His jaw dropped and his face flushed. "Oh. Shit."

I pressed my finger to my lips to quiet them. "You're forgiven if you tell me where in there my husband-to-be is hiding," I whispered.

Harzix closed his eyes and concentrated. I've always been a little jealous of pixie ESP. "Keep going," he replied softly. "There's a small break room with a cot in the next corner. He's in there...and he's not alone."

"Good," I replied. He flinched in surprise. "I'm hoping to catch him in the act."

The pixie blushed again. "If I'm reading things right, Your Highness, you're right on time."

"Excellent. I'll see to it you're given time and a half for your service today."

Now he looked genuinely confused. "Thank you, Your Highness."

Rather than continue along beside the tent, I quickly jogged a good twenty paces further out into the courtyard. A few dozen more steps toward the castle wall put the corner of the tent directly between me and the rest of the party—exactly the angle I needed. I paused to make sure I had everything lined up carefully. I was a football kicker setting up for a game-winning field goal, a pool shark carefully calculating a quick bank around the eight ball, a model gazing out upon a gorgeous runway flanked with paparazzi, my father at a bacon sampling convention: I had my target in my sights, I knew my path was true, and all I had to do was follow through properly.

It's dawned on me, Diary, that I haven't explained the method behind my madness. It's simple, really: Twat Face Jr.'s scumbag tendencies enabled me to take one of the greatest controls the patriarchy had foisted upon its princesses and deploy that burden as a weapon against one of its own. Ever wonder how the king guarantees that the princess only ever gets knocked up by the man to whom he sells her? There's magic for that, passed down from mother to daughter for generations. Like all Talvayan princesses, I come equipped with ABS.

Gritting my teeth and clenching my fists, I charged the back corner of the tent like a bull aiming for the metaphorical china shop. Luckily I'd worn sensible-ish shoes. I threw myself against the side of the tent and kind of bounced off. That canvas was thicker than it looked. It kept a sixty-pound princess at bay, but it couldn't stop the ridiculous magic a bunch of ancient douchebags built into her genetic code. The screams of Sorrin and his mate told me all I needed to know. Quansea later told me through a very effusive email that they were hurled through the opposite side of the tent, spiraled through the air, and crashed into one of the metal tree pieces right in the middle of the engagement party. Bare ass. Mid-coitus. Covered in spilled liquor and shattered glass. Quansea couldn't have been happier.

ABS, by the way, is the Anti-Boner Shield. Any male who gets a little too excited too close to yours truly is immediately expelled from the premises at a speed best described as "uh-oh." This would have made middle school dances *super* awkward if

I had gone to any. The royal wedding ceremony binds the new king to the land, but it's also an elaborate piece of sorcery that grants the groom immunity to the ABS. Ridiculous, right? The best sorcerers in Talvayne thousands of years ago had the power to protect their princesses in perpetuity and that's how they did it. Priorities.

I pulled myself up off the ground and dusted myself off. The pixies nearby gave me a floating ovation. I bowed once and strutted happily to the nearest entrance to the keep. My work there was done.

— CHAPTER FIVE —

In a small but immaculately clean public ladies' room off the archives of the Palace of Light, a steady trickle of water rained down through the vent in the ceiling. Rather than puddling across the white and black tile floor, the droplets settled atop each other in two distinct piles about a foot apart. The two stacks slowly formed toes, then ankles, then calves and thighs. Myrindi's torso appeared where the legs met, then grew up and outward into arms, hands, a neck, and a head topped with shoulder-length hair. The water solidified into blue flesh, firm and solid and pricked with goose pimples.

"Fuck, it's cold," the princess muttered as she strode into one of the room's two stalls. The real problem with liquifying yourself, she mused, is that you can't take your damn clothes with you when you do it. Although the toilet seat looked perfectly clean, she still covered it with half a dozen paper liners from the dispenser on the wall. She sat and proceeded to take the most satisfying piss of her entire life.

"But now what?" she mumbled. When she'd agreed to make a run for it, she'd failed to consider just how boring hanging out in a bathroom by herself would be. And what if someone other than Fro and the others found her first? The logical reaction, she supposed, would be to liquify and hide in one of the toilets, but Talvayan Crown Princesses don't do such things. Toilet water is for gutter trash like her old playmate, Nella.

Someone in the stall to her left unleashed a tremendous fart that echoed through the room. Myrindi froze and covered her mouth, trying not to gag at the stench. Did whoever-it-was know she was there? As if in answer, a slender hand reached gently underneath the stall's wall.

"Spare some paper?" a smooth, confident voice asked.

"Rayn!" Myrindi shouted happily as she passed over her stall's spare roll. "You would *not* believe the uncool shit I've been through today."

"Let me guess: Sorrin and Gaptorix staged a coup and murdered your father, and you were rescued by a trio of mercenaries who picked the wrong janitor's closet to hide in."

"Pretty much."

"Everything's going according to plan, then."

Incredulous, Myrindi frowned. The gills in her neck rippled angrily. "Um...what?"

"He's started rounding up and killing the Conclave of Kings, too. Wasn't sure he had the walnuts for that part. Probably Gaptorix's influence."

"Hold on a minute, sister. Square with me here. I thought we were besties."

Rayn giggled like a five-year-old girl who'd just been handed a hot fudge sundae the size of her head. "Myrindi, I swear to you that everything going down right now is purely in your best interest."

"I'm naked and I'm stuck in a fucking bathroom!"

In response, a brown suitcase slid across the floor and into Myrindi's stall. It stopped at the princess's feet and flipped open. Inside were a pair of jeans, a T-shirt, a set of underwear, a pair of running sneakers, and a red and yellow pinwheel on a white plastic stick.

"I've always thought you look best in black," Rayn said. "Goes great with your skin tone."

Myrindi eyed the contents of the suitcase warily. "'All according to plan,' huh? Couldn't you have planned something a little more glamorous?"

"Stilettos aren't much good for running from angry trolls."

"Ugh, does there have to be more running?"

"Running is the primary activity of people who are on the run, so...yes."

The princess sighed and shook her head in frustration. "Can't you just get me out of here? We could go on vacation, take a road trip, maybe check out the catwalks in Paris..."

"I'd like nothing better, Myrindi, but that wouldn't get us anywhere. All I can do is position the appropriate people in the appropriate places and cross my fingers. If it helps at all...I'm usually not wrong about these things." The toilet flushed. "Catch you later, bestie. Pike will be here in fifteen minutes or so. Tell him I said hi!"

Desperate, Myrindi sprang to her feet, burst out of the stall, and kicked in the door to Rayn's. It was empty. And there was plenty of toilet paper.

Dear Diary,

This day just keeps getting better. Now not only am I stuck in a bathroom, waiting to be saved by an idiot neanderthal, I'm also dressed like a clueless suburban mom about to sneak out of the house for a midnight rendezvous with some dude who lives up the block. Would a pair of earrings have been too much to ask for? I thought I taught Rayn better than that. We've spent so many late nights giggling over fashion mags and red carpet specials that I assumed she'd learned a few things. Guess you don't always know your bestie as well as you think.

All that crap about a plan is a little disconcerting, too. Rayn's one of the best schemers in the business, and it never stops; you can almost see the neurons in her pretty head firing like a machine gun through her dark, heavy eyes. She connects causes with effects quicker than anyone I've ever met, but that may not be saying much given that I've mostly been exposed to boot-licking sycophants and inbred nobility. I'm going to guess that she didn't spirit me away to safety because she needs me in Talvayne to do something, although I've got no clue what. I really should've asked what this fucking pinwheel is for. I'll just have to trust her. I've got good reason to trust her. Without Rayn, we wouldn't be having this conversation.

It was a sunny day about six months after I ruined Sorrin's night at our engagement party. I hadn't seen the little stump since, and Father had been leaving me alone—which probably accounted for the awesome weather. It was Tuesday afternoon, so I was tanning in my favorite spot out in the Glittering Gardens: beside the fig trees at the very edge of the veranda, overlooking the Roaring Falls of Rabitna as they dumped billions of gallons of water down a terraced cliffside into the peaceful Faldahadron River below. The falls are a little loud, but I'm a water nymph so I love that fucking sound, all right? Fro really likes it out there too. He sits right on the edge, his legs dangling over the side, and he whittles all sorts of little boats, birds, and animals. I wore my super cute blue bikini and my newest aviators, and I'd brought my backlog of *Entertainment Weekly* and *Rolling Stone* so I'd have something to do if I got tired of sleeping and drinking. Pippa, my handmaiden, kept me supplied with a steady stream of secretly-non-virgin virgin cucumber mojitos. There are definite benefits to staying on the servants' good side, which really isn't all that hard given how much they all hate Lard Ass. Yes, I was still just ten, but keep in mind that I'm naturally very good at manipulating the chemicals in my body. Sweating out a little rum ain't no thing.

After my fourth mojito, however, I began to feel a bit sluggish. Not I'm-ten-and-I've-been-drinking-for-three-hours sluggish, mind you, but something's-really-not-right sluggish. I felt like my insides weren't moving correctly, like my flesh had somehow become denser. I tried to sit up, but a wave of dizziness knocked me right back down. "Fro," I croaked. My throat was the driest it's ever been and my tongue felt like it was made of granite. I couldn't open my gills. "I think I've been poisoned."

He didn't stop to question me. "You're a most unhealthy shade of gray, Your Highness," he said somberly as he scooped me into his arms. He shifted me a bit so he could reach down and grab the remains of my most recent drink between his fingertips. "Let's go see Dr. Neltsin."

My temperature rose alarmingly as Fro carried me through the Glittering Gardens toward the back side of the palace. I tried to force myself to sweat—normally an easy task—and found I couldn't. That was the scariest part of all. I'd been sick briefly before, but my ability to regulate my body's fluids meant I'd always gotten over anything I caught pretty quickly. This was something different. Whoever poisoned me knew exactly what he or she was doing.

We passed Pippa on the way. "Anything strange in the kitchen?" Fro asked her quickly.

"N-n-nothing," she stammered. She sounded genuinely surprised, but I was in no condition to make such judgments. Fro continued on, apparently satisfied that Pippa had done nothing wrong.

Dr. Neltsin, who'd been there for my birth and had tended to me all my life, kept an office in the basement of the palace.

Fro descended the spiral staircase at breakneck speed, adding a bit of vertigo to my expanding list of symptoms. It was all I could do to refrain from vomiting on his chest. You're welcome, Fro. Anyway, I've never liked visiting Neltsin. Number one, he's a crusty old gnoll with teeth like a rusted bear trap and body odor that suggests he somehow bathes in the Rot every morning. Number two, he has no concept of personal space. He's a notorious close talker, a trait which only exacerbates the issues I mentioned previously. Number three, his offices are like some movie villain's weird science lab. Every wall is covered in shelves containing jars full of crap I don't want to think about, some of it still alive. Rumor has it he practices necromancy and other forms of magical science typically frowned upon by polite society. Rumor also has it he sleeps in his offices and routinely fornicates with the contents of some of his jars. At the time, he was undeniably the best physician in Talvayne, however, so Father and the kings let him be.

The infirmary door was locked. Fro knocked it down with one solid kick. Dr. Neltsin's assistant, a prim young water nymph in a white nurse's uniform who moved like she had a three-foot pole perpetually shoved up her ass, rose from her seat behind her desk as if to admonish us, then stopped suddenly when she realized who we were. She reached down to a panel atop her desk and pressed an intercom button with one slender finger. "Dr. Neltsin, Princess Myrindi to see you. Immediately."

"I'll take her in the OR," Dr. Neltsin's voice buzzed back.

In hindsight we both should've been suspicious of our destination, but Fro was sick with worry and I was just plain sick. Fro carried me through the double doors to our right and into a long hallway trimmed with Dr. Neltsin's specimens, several of which I swear made eye contact with me as we passed. I'm pretty sure one severed hand floating in a jar of reddish fluid flashed me the shocker, but I may have been hallucinating at that point.

Fro burst into the operating room and laid me gently on the table under a harsh fluorescent light. I hadn't been in this room since the day I was born. Although I knew it was my destiny to return here someday to bear a daughter of my own, I can't say I was particularly thrilled to see it again. Dr. Neltsin entered through a side door, crouching low to squeeze all nine feet of himself through the regular-sized door. He's been Royal Physician for the last hundred years or so and I don't really understand why he doesn't remodel the place so he fits. Maybe he likes making an entrance.

"Out," he snapped, slipping blue latex gloves onto his huge hands. "I'll take it from here."

Fro offered Dr. Neltsin the remainder of my mojito. "She claims she was poisoned."

The Royal Physician glowered at him, his beady little eyes almost comically small in his hairy horse face. A creature as big and ugly as Dr. Neltsin really has no business in a white medical smock. He should've chosen something more flattering, perhaps with a vertical pinstripe to make him appear thinner. "I don't need that to tell me she's ingested a thickener."

"Fine," Fro sighed. "Fix her up. I'm going to find whoever did this and rip out his throat."

The troll spun on his heel and stomped back out into the hallway. Dr. Neltsin locked the door behind him. "Sure you are."

"What's a thickener?" I squeaked. My mouth and tongue really, really didn't want to move. Forcing them to do so took a concerted effort and kind of hurt.

Dr. Neltsin covered the seven or so feet between the door and the prep counter in the corner with one long stride. "A thickener is a mixture of minerals, enchanted just so, which neutralizes a water nymph's natural ability to control his or her bodily fluids and hence removes the ability to liquify. Side effects include fever, aching muscles, decreased range of motion, dry mouth, and near paralysis. It's typically employed by rapists, murderers, and surgeons. After all, your kind is a bit difficult to slice into when you're all...watery."

His description was less than reassuring. I wanted Fro back, but I was too proud to say so. And I couldn't even cry because my body wouldn't let me. "Dangerous?" I asked. "Permanent?"

"Not really," he replied as he rummaged through the stainless steel cabinets on the wall. "It'll pass on its own in an hour or so."

I didn't understand. Why would someone dose me with something like that? Was it just a practical joke? Were Sorrin and my jackass father trying to get some small revenge for how I'd repeatedly embarrassed them? It made no sense.

Dr. Neltsin turned and smiled, showing off his fangs and all his pointy, crooked teeth. In one hand he carried an ice pick. The other clutched a rubber mallet. "Should be more than enough time to do what we need to do."

I have never been so fucking scared in my entire life. I would've pissed myself if I could have. I forced myself to try to get up, but I couldn't move. The thickener had fully kicked in.

"Figured it out, have you?" Dr. Neltsin muttered as he closed the distance between us with a single giant step and ducked his vile head under the fluorescent light. He smelled like dog shit. "You're not my first, by the way. We're forced to lobotomize every third or fourth princess. Although I am a bit out of practice; haven't had to do one of these since your great-grandma. If it were up to me, we'd give you all a little love tap at birth. Guess the kings get better prices from prospective suitors when you're whole."

I was forced to watch in horror, paralyzed, as he lifted my right eyelid with his sharpened fingernail and slid the cold metal of the ice pick between the top of my eye and its socket. "Fro!" I tried to scream, although it came out as little more than a terrified gasp.

"Now, some people prefer to do this through magical means," he said as he lined up the mallet with his other hand. "They say it's more 'humane,' somehow less 'barbaric.' Bullshit, I say. One way or the other, you're breaking someone's brain in an attempt to create a more docile, reasonable individual—and what could do a better job of making someone fall in line than the memory of an ice pick through the ol' eye socket, eh?"

I braced myself. This was it, then, the end of my little crusade of disobedience against the gutless turd burglars running this place. No more strolls into the Rot. No more telling my father to lay off the cake. No more insisting that I wanted the red fucking dress, not the yellow fucking skirt. No more rainstorms because I didn't want to ride in Lard Ass's stupid carriage. No more launching my fiancé with anti-boner magic. No more pursuing my mother's goal of making all the assholes who'd held generations of us down as miserable as all the princesses have been. No more Myrindi, really. I hoped I'd at least manage to retain my fashion sense. I'd never forgive Dr. Neltsin if I suddenly developed a taste for wearing sandals with socks or traipsing around in cargo pants.

Before the blow could come, the ugly gnoll was flung across the room into the cabinets from which he'd retrieved his implements. He bounced off and landed on his ass with a meaty thud. The mallet and ice pick fell from his slack grip. For a moment I wondered if he'd gotten a little too excited with the idea of vandalizing my brains, but I knew that couldn't be right.

The slender woman who opened the locked door and sauntered into the operating room as if she owned the place was the most beautiful thing I'd ever seen. She didn't have much of a figure, but she somehow filled that tight black dress with the presence of a girl with double Ds and a rockin' ass. Jet-black hair billowed out behind her like it had a mind of its own. The harsh fluorescents didn't do her pale skin any favors, but even in that light I could tell she'd broken her fair share of hearts—and probably other things, like bones and spleens. Something about her was a bit off.

"Who the fuck are you?" Dr. Neltsin stammered from the floor.

She smiled a smile full of perfect white teeth dripping with enough malice to strip the paint off a car. "I'm what becomes of oppressed little magic girls who get tired of bullshit like this." Poetry to my ears. I immediately wanted to be this woman's friend.

Dr. Neltsin snorted as he shifted onto one knee and then pushed himself to his feet. "I'll have you know this operation was ordered by the King of Talvayne himself! You have no right to interfere!"

She stuck out her tongue and gave him a raspberry, then magically shoved him right back into the cabinets with a gentle flick of her fingers.

Dr. Neltsin's eyes went wide as he shook his head back and forth to clear his vision. "I'm going to call the guards—"

"No, you're not," she replied, her dark eyes glittering with amusement. "You're going to tell me how I can fix the princess."

The doctor opened his mouth to call the guards, but a snap of her fingers and his lips slammed shut.

She sighed in mock disappointment. "Fine. If there has to be an operation, there has to be an operation. Scalpel?"

A drawer beside Dr. Neltsin's head burst open. A trio of scalpels, their sharp tips shining wickedly, floated up into the air to hover inches from the Royal Physician's ugly horse face.

"W-water!" he shouted, his eyes darting frantically between the blades. "Lots and lots of water!"

The knobs on the tiny sink behind him spun open, unleashing a torrent from the spigot. The woman turned to me. "Focus on that water and *pull*."

I did just as she instructed. Never had I wanted anything so badly in my life. At first the stream of water merely bent toward me as if diverted by a strong breeze, but then the entire thing whipped across the room and between my chapped lips. I drank greedily, my gills pulsing with relief. Tap water had never tasted so good. Don't tell anyone.

The woman came to stand beside me. She brushed her soft fingers across my forehead in a gesture somehow both comforting and eerie. "They didn't tell you about that, did they? Probably because it works on people, too."

I shook my head gently so as not to interrupt the water's flow. I felt stronger and more like myself every second, and I could feel my temperature dropping rapidly.

"It's a nymph thing, like being able to liquify yourself," she added. "I assume you figured that one out on your own?"

I nodded. She spoke to me like I was a real person, not like I was a product to sell or a thing that needed protection and guidance. No one had really done that since Mother. It was... nice.

"Spoiled old men in positions of power tend to leave out the important parts," she said. "Can't have anything rocking their gold-plated yachts."

Satisfied, I released my grip on the water. The stream recoiled back into its proper position, dropping a small puddle across the floor as it did so. "Or interrupting dessert," I replied as I sat up. My throat was still a little dry, but I really, really wanted to talk to my rescuer. "Who are you?"

"My name's Rayn," she replied. "When I heard what you pulled in the Rot, I just had to meet you. Everybody's talking about it."

"Everybody?"

"*Everybody*. Nice bit of work, that."

"Thanks. Did you hear about that time I launched my cheating fiancé and his strumpet of the day into a giant metal tree with my vagina shield?"

Rayn giggled, a sound like a cool breeze on a warm summer's day. "Next time, try lighting him on fire."

"I was saving that for the honeymoon."

"Talk about heating up the bedroom."

"Hey, anything to kindle a bit of romance."

"There's nothing quite like fiery passion."

"I sleep better in a warm bed anyway."

"What in the fuck are you two going on about?" Dr. Neltsin growled from the corner. Rayn and I had become such fast friends that we'd forgotten about him. Though the three scalpels still lingered near his face, he'd turned angry and defiant. I don't think he really took Rayn seriously, like she was just some temporary inconvenience he'd be rid of soon.

"So about this guy," she said. "What do we do with him? Your call."

I turned my attention to the Royal Physician. He glowered back at me as if he somehow thought he were still in control of the situation. I suppose that's just what good sycophants do; even when the supposed authority backing up their heinous acts is proven impotent, they cling to it desperately because it's all they've ever known. A more philosophical princess might've used that as an excuse for mercy. I simply chalked that line of thought up to a few stray neurons firing too fast due to stress. "You know what they say, Rayn: a frontal lobe for a frontal lobe."

But the trio of scalpels clattered to the floor. Dr. Neltsin sighed with relief and stood up. "Thank you, my dear. Such a punishment would be far too harsh to inflict upon a humble physician merely attempting to do his job."

Why hadn't Rayn sent those blades straight through his eye sockets and into his skull to scramble his gray matter? Before I could protest, the big gnoll's body went rigid and he floated a few inches up into the air.

"Who said you were off the hook?" Rayn asked curiously. "Oh, those scalpels certainly would've done the trick, but I'm curious about something you said earlier. You remember that part about a magical lobotomy being more humane and somehow less barbaric? I'd like to test that hypothesis."

Dr. Neltsin's body spasmed and his eyes rolled back in his dumb horse head. I smiled evilly, savoring the stupid gnoll's every twitch as Rayn fed a portion of his brain to her telekinetic blender. Saliva bubbled out from the corners of his mouth and trickled down his chin. Twenty seconds or so after it started, Rayn tossed him backwards into the cabinets one more time for good measure. On the floor, he pulled himself into the fetal position and squealed in pain.

"What do you think, Myrindi?" Rayn asked. "More humane? Less barbaric?"

"Hmm. It's all the same to me."

"Yeah. Sucks either way."

"I was just catching some rays out in the Glittering Gardens. Care to join me?"

"I don't tan, sister, I just burn. Besides...I think it's time we pay your father a visit."

"Oooooooh, I like the way you think."

And just like that, we were besties. You know how it goes.

— CHAPTER SIX —

T he ladies' room door eased open with just the barest sound of squeaking hinges. "Little bitch?" Pike whispered tentatively. "You in here?"

"No," Myrindi replied. She stood up on the toilet seat to peer over the top of the stall. "Hey, there's a turd in this shitter that looks a lot like you."

Pike rolled his eyes. "Then congratulations, Your Highness, you just met the handsomest dump on the planet. Let's go."

"The hell happened to you?" she asked as she exited the stall. Pike was covered in a sheen of sweat and dust. Dents pocked his red plate armor.

"Trolls," he replied. "We burst out of that closet and took the fight to 'em. We had the bastards, too, until the big one showed up."

"No shirt? Super stylish loincloth?"

"That's the guy. Friend of yours?"

"Gaptorix. He's a twat."

"Well, that twat managed to hold all four of us off at once for two whole minutes. We had him surrounded, and then he clapped his hands and brought the ceiling down on everybody—his own wounded included. Nasty son of a bitch."

"Is it just you?"

"I got out of the way. The others didn't. Figured it was about time to collect you and get the fuck out of here."

Myrindi wrinkled her nose. "You don't think Fro, Lep, and Chas..."

He shook his head. "No, I don't think they're dead. Takes a lot more than one ceiling to kill my pals, and that troll of yours is a tough bastard. They'll link up with us if they can. Now let's go."

"Oh—by the way, Rayn says hi."

Pike froze. "That's where you got those clothes?"

Myrindi nodded and tapped her hip. "And this fucking pinwheel." She'd stuck it in her belt.

"What's it do?"

"No clue."

"Uh-huh. Careful with that."

The narrow hallway outside was empty. Myrindi wrinkled her nose at the dull gray paint on the walls and the industrial white tile on the floor. Pike led the way, ready to pounce at the first sign of trouble, while the princess shuffled along behind him with her hands in her pockets. She paused to examine the fire extinguisher built into the wall as Pike peered tentatively around the corner.

"Keep up!" he hissed back at her.

"I'm happy to keep my distance until you get a shower," she said haughtily. He responded by wiping a few fingers of sweat from his brow and flicking it in her direction. She cringed away and squealed. "Dirty fucking elf—"

In the distance, a door slammed open. "Spread out," a deep, gravelly voice commanded. "They're in here somewhere."

Myrindi quickly scampered closer to Pike. "Gaptorix!" she whispered. "What do we do?"

"Stay low, stay close, stay quiet—just don't be you. If they spot us, run away and don't look back."

The princess nodded. Pike crept slowly around the corner into the main floor of the archives with Myrindi right on his heels. Storehouse for all of Talvayne's collected knowledge, the archives were essentially a huge library the width and length of a football field. Row after row after row of tightly packed shelves sprouted up from the wooden floor like blades of grass reaching up toward the gray ceiling four stories above. There were plenty of books, sure, but Talvayne's denizens had never been the sort to always do things the easy way. Huge chunks of the collection consisted of stone tablets, ropes tied into strands of knots, wind chimes meant to be played at certain frequencies, dried fruit arranged in intricate pictograms, and huge collections of sand, leaves, hair, and feces that supposedly had yet to be properly translated. The first row of shelves Pike and the princess took cover behind was full of tree stumps carved with the blocky letters of troll love poetry.

"Wait a minute," the princess hissed. "'Just don't be you?' *Really?*"

Pike clamped his hand down tightly over her mouth. "This is neither the time nor the place, Your Royalness." She bit down hard on the elf's middle finger, but he didn't even flinch.

Several dozen yards behind them, another door slammed open. "West entrance secured, sir," a deep troll voice bellowed. Pike swore under his breath and let go of the princess. She stuck her pink tongue out at him.

"Well done," Gaptorix replied. He cleared his throat. "Princess Myrindi! We know you and at least one of your protectors is here in the archives. We have every entrance secured. Surrender and I will suggest that King Sorrin show mercy to your allies. Make us hunt you down and we will kill all we find with you."

Myrindi smirked at Pike. "Oh, there's a fucking threat," she whispered. "So how are you going to get me out of here?"

The elf scowled. "We know they've got the two obvious exits covered. Know any others?"

It was Myrindi's turn to look angry. "I am a Talvayan Crown Princess. I sit in my parlor, I attend fancy parties with important dignitaries, I sun myself in the gardens, and I get a mani-pedi twice a week. I do not visit dumpy old libraries full of crap the average flea market would reject."

"I know a way out," a small voice squeaked. A tiny girl looked out at them from the bottom shelf a few feet to their left, worming her slender body between a pair of thick rocks covered in white and blue gnomish pictograms. She was a sand nymph, but her gritty features didn't distort the gentle lines of her young face. Wispy brown hair tumbled from her head in tight, frizzy curls. Her glassy white eyes, devoid of pupils, roiled like clouds in a hurricane.

Pike shuffled a few steps closer to the sand nymph, putting himself between the newcomer and the princess. "Who are you?"

"My name is Gol," she replied. "I'm the apprentice to Reften, Talvayne's Master Archivist. I can get us out using the service elevator to the loading docks. We move things in and out using a hidden space under the floor. No one really knows about it except me and Reften. We'll be safe."

As Pike considered Gol's offer, Myrindi darted around the big elf. "You swear fealty to Crown Princess Myrindi, true heir to the Throne of Light, and you promise to piss on the grave of Sorrin the Pretender once my muscle over here tears his ugly little puppet head from his stupid wooden body?"

Gol replied with a deep bow, an oddly snakelike motion given the way she lay on the floor. "With all my heart, Your Highness."

"I like you," Myrindi said. "You shall have jewels, gold, and an expensive makeover when this is all over."

"Thank you, Your Highness." Gol wriggled the rest of the way out of the shelf and stood. She wore a simple brown dress and a pair of leather sandals. Myrindi turned her nose up at both. "This way, please."

"I am not your muscle," Pike growled.

"You're right," the princess replied. "You're my asshole."

Dear Diary,

I'm still not sure you can hear me, but whatever. Thinking at you takes my mind off the fact that I'm now stuck in a dry, dreary loading dock with an elf who's got a raging case of fucking jackass. We're going to wait until evening to make our escape from the palace, per Lep's original plan. Gol's off looking for Fro and the others. She locked the door up tight and she's got the only key. We should be fine for a couple hours. In the meantime...want to know what happened when Rayn and I went to visit my father after he tried to have the Royal Physician julienne my frontal lobe? I know you do.

We found Lard Ass in—where else?—the dining hall. Like pretty much every other room in the palace, it's a long, tall, cavernous space designed to hold large numbers of people. Trimmed with a glittering hardwood floor, walls inlaid with gold and silver murals depicting heroes and battles of Talvayne's past, and a glass ceiling that somehow softens the sun's rays but warms cool moonlight, the dining hall has played host to countless balls, banquets, rallies, remembrances, and receptions. It's Talvayne's premiere event space. Lard Ass, of course, liked to use it for lunches alone or occasionally with a few of his favorite toadies. Sometimes he would just go in there and laugh and listen to the echoes. He's not that bright.

My father sat in his usual place at the center of the Royal Family's table on the raised dais at the west end of the dining hall. The table, a black and gold granite monstrosity that ran the width of the room, was piled high with a variety of meats and cheeses that must've wiped out at least three farms. It was like the charcuterie board from hell. Sorrin sat at the first table in front of the dais, right in front of my father but quite obviously beneath the king. Personally, if I had been sitting in Lard Ass's chair and wanted to make Twat Face Jr.'s position relative to my own known, I would've made the ugly little stump sit in a pile of mud and shit outside. A trio of pixies—two glowing green, one blue—flitted to and fro to deliver food to the two conspirators.

Lard Ass's mouth dropped when he saw Rayn and me walk through the nearby entrance. A slice of half-eaten sopressata oozed out through his fat lips and dropped onto his plate with an audible splat. "Myrindi? Is everything all right, my dear? Who's this woman with you?"

Twat Face Jr. turned in his seat to look at us. His face went pale. On a wood nymph, that's like a piece of dark oak suddenly turning into a much lighter hunk of pine. I winked at him and waved excitedly.

"I don't think you'll have any more trouble with the Royal Physician," Rayn said calmly, ruffling the leaves on Sorrin's head with her fingers as she strolled past.

"Trouble?" Lard Ass burbled. "Why, Dr. Neltsin is one of the most loyal and able members of my staff!"

I took a seat next to Sorrin and gave him a friendly pat on the knee. He looked like he wanted to melt into the floor. Rayn continued on and stepped up onto the dais. I couldn't help feeling like she belonged up there. The three pixies stopped flitting and hung still at the far end of the table, watching intently.

"That's exactly the sort of trouble I mean," Rayn replied. "That sort of loyalty simply won't do. It blinds us to what's really right and what's terribly wrong."

Lard Ass glanced down at me and then back at the intruder who'd dared interrupt his lunch. "You speak in riddles, woman. You have three seconds to tell me who you are and what you want before I call the guard."

"I'm your daughter's new best friend. I want what's best for her." She picked up a slice of prosciutto, sniffed it disdainfully, and tossed it over her shoulder to the floor.

"Really? I'm Myrindi's father and the King of Talvayne!" Lard Ass bellowed. "I *know* what's best for her!"

Rayn wrinkled her nose. "I don't think you do."

Father's jowls jiggled angrily. "I will not be slandered in my own palace. Guards!"

Gaptorix burst in through a hidden door in the wall behind the Royal Table, snorting and flexing his pecs in all his mostly-naked glory. "You called, sire?"

"Remove this pest!"

"Yes, Gaptorix," Rayn added, pointing to Sorrin. "Please do something about this ridiculous shrub that thinks it's going to penetrate the princess."

The big troll looked around in confusion. His species has never been particularly skilled at processing multiple inputs. No offense, Fro.

That brought Twat Face Jr. to his feet. "What exactly is your issue with me?" he asked. "We've never even met."

Rayn spun to face him, one hand planted firmly on her narrow hip. "Assholes like you are all the same," she snarled. "Meet one and you meet them all."

"The same could be said about uppity lunatics like you," Sorrin spat. "Recognize your betters, learn your place, and stay in it!"

She smiled. "Oh, I know my place. It's everywhere rules and tradition have created stagnant cultures rife with corruption. It's everywhere I can facilitate change with a few words or simple, direct action. I am exactly where I should be right now." Sure, she's a little melodramatic, but hot damn she's the best.

"Enough!" Lard Ass burbled. "Gaptorix!"

Rayn giggled and snapped her fingers. A tiny flame blossomed to life between the floorboards at Sorrin's feet. The wood nymph leapt backwards in alarm, but the fire spread to surround him before he could escape. Gaptorix had taken a few steps toward Rayn but stopped when he realized what she was up to.

Twat Face Jr. somehow choked back his fear and remained defiant. "Release me!"

"Answer me oooooooooooooooooone simple question first," she replied. "Whose idea was it to task the honorable Dr. Neltsin with rooting around in young Myrindi's lovely little brain?"

The wood nymph thought for a moment, then thrust his chin forward haughtily. "It was my idea, you bitch. The princess is in need of a serious attitude adjustment. Do you have any idea how difficult she's made my life? Do you have any idea how difficult she's made *her father's* life? And I'm supposed to marry that?" He punctuated that last line with a derisive snort.

On the outside, I smiled. Mission accomplished, right? But on the inside...I don't know. Sorrin's disgusting, but his words still hurt. My mother had neglected to mention that frustrating all the people who wanted to control me would also make them hate me, and I'd never put two and two together on my own. In a way, that admission proved I—and I mean Myrindi the young girl, not the Crown Princess of Talvayne—was worth even less to them than I thought. I'd always pictured myself as a sort of prize they were all fighting for, but that couldn't have been further from the truth. I was just a burden that came with a title and some fancy magic. The real prize was the combination of money, fame, and influence that came from marrying me.

I glanced up at my father. He was staring not at Rayn or Sorrin, but right down at yours truly. I've never seen a look tinged with so much hatred. *Fuck you, too!* I thought, though my mouth wouldn't form the words. Yeah, I know he'd been complicit with and perhaps even looking forward to the attempt to lobotomize me, but somehow this was infinitely more personal. He hadn't been the one actually wielding the ice pick, you know? Maybe I just hadn't really wanted to believe my own father capable of such a thing. In my head he'd always just been a big, harmless doofus who probably loved me deep down because I was his daughter, damn it. That vision of him was gone. Fuck you, Diary.

"Whaddaya think, Myrindi?" Rayn asked, one eyebrow raised. "Should I roast him, or should I let him go? He's your fiancé. I don't really care either way."

I could feel the three men in the room staring holes through me. On the one hand, if anyone deserved to be burned alive, it was certainly that stupid little stump. Just his dumb face had always made me want to go get a box of matches. On the other hand...that was exactly the sort of shit they would've pulled if our roles were reversed. I wanted to beat them, but I wanted to do it on my terms. Shredding Dr. Neltsin's brain instead of finding a better way to deal with him had maybe been a mistake. Whoopsies.

"What did you trade for my hand in marriage?" I asked sternly.

"Two hundred goats, the Sword of Renticulus, and my family's holdings in Ambershire," Sorrin replied. He hesitated, then continued. "Your grandfather got five times that for your mother, but you're...damaged goods."

Livestock, a pretty knife, and some real estate on the outskirts of town with a lovely view of the Rot. "Renounce the deal and you can go," I snapped.

"Done," he said before I'd even finished. "Gladly. Being king is not worth this shit."

The ring of fire surrounding the wood nymph went *wumpf* and disappeared. Thin tendrils of smoke wafted up from the unharmed floorboards. Sorrin turned on his heel and scampered from the room.

"Myrindi!" Lard Ass bellowed, clearly ready to launch into another tirade.

I cut him off before he could get going. "You can find a better deal, Father," I snapped. "I'm worth a hell of a lot more than what Twat Face Jr. was offering. How about a yacht that spits out smaller yachts? Or a helicopter made of solid gold?"

"Maybe a chocolate waterfall," Rayn suggested.

"Ooooh, I like the way you think, girlfriend. How about an emerald jacuzzi with a built-in bar and soft-serve ice cream maker?"

"Or a sports car that turns into a hovercraft."

"Or a full-sized replica of the space shuttle filled with Paris's hottest fashions."

"Or a lifetime of guaranteed hit singles."

"Or a food processor that turns carrots into hundred-dollar bills."

"Or a five-movie deal with the option to direct."

"Or—"

My father silenced us by slamming his fist on the table. I'd never seen him so flustered. He'd turned a shade of purple usually reserved for singing dinosaurs. His eyes bulged so far out of his head that I had to wonder if they were trying to escape. "Just *what* in the name of Axzar are you two going on about?"

My BFF and I traded annoyed glances. "You know what he really should trade you for?" Rayn asked.

"No! Do tell!"

"A personality and a Stairmaster."

"*Enough!*" Lard Ass shrieked. "Gaptorix! I thought I instructed you to remove this witch!"

"Aww, so you have heard of me!" Rayn chirped. No one got her joke. Turns out most of the nonhumans in the world know her simply as the Witch. Capital W. She's a big deal. Like, should be hosting three reality shows and selling her own line of perfume big, except she's pissed off so many people that she'll never get the chance to take her rightful place as a cultural icon. No joke.

Gaptorix stomped forward, finally focused on removing the intruder upon whom he'd been unleashed. He didn't get very far. Rayn snapped her fingers and sent a salami from the table careening into the big troll's beefy face. He shrugged the light blow off with a snarl and kept coming. Rayn snapped her fingers again. This time, every piece of meat lifted into the air, hovered for a moment, and then rocketed away to pummel Gaptorix's face and torso. He tried to fight off the barrage with his hands, but the torrent of meat was too much for one man to fight off. He went down in a pile of cold cuts, sausages, and pepperoni.

"Oops," Rayn quipped. "Forgot the cheese!"

One more snap of her fingers, and then that piled on top of Gaptorix too. Father just gaped at her, slack-jawed and petrified, as she slithered onto the suddenly empty table and took his chubby cheeks in her slender fingers.

"You're going to be good to my girl," she said softly. "You aren't going to damage a single hair on her precious head. You're going to find her a harmless husband who will treat her right. Do you know why you're going to do these things?"

Tears welled up in Lard Ass's eyes. "Because if I don't, you'll be back," he croaked.

She smiled at him and slapped his jowls playfully. "You're smarter than you look." She spun around and favored me with a friendly wink. "See you soon, sis."

And then she was gone. No finger snap, no puff of smoke—nothing. It was as if she'd never been there.

Deciding she had the right idea, I turned and headed back to my chambers. I mostly stayed there for the next six years. Father visited rarely and included me in his various social responsibilities even less, although he always made sure to trot me out for an hour or two at important events just to keep up appearances. From that day on, he always looked at me as if he thought I was about to walk up and shank him. I now know what it's like to be the baddest man in prison.

But life wasn't terrible. Rayn kept her promise. She came to visit every week or two. She brought magazines and DVDs and enough gossip to keep my head spinning. Like I said: we're besties.

— CHAPTER SEVEN —

Why are you staring at me?" Myrindi asked.

Pike shrugged. He'd shucked his bright red armor so he could sit comfortably in the big leather office chair. Behind him, a trio of grimy glass panes overlooked the palace's empty loading dock. He looked a bit like a scuba diver in the black lycra he wore underneath the heavy plate. "I'm trying to figure you out."

The princess lay on the couch a few feet away. She didn't approve of the upholstery's floral pattern, but it was comfortable enough for now. "I'm the Crown Princess of Talvayne. I live a life of luxury few can even dream of. Someday I will give birth to the next Crown Princess, and then I will die. There's nothing to figure out."

Pike swung his big bare feet up onto the metal desk, carelessly scattering papers and writing implements. "I'm not so sure about that."

Myrindi rolled her eyes and glared up at the suspended ceiling. Looking at the old tiles, yellowed with years of cigarette smoke, was better than looking at the big, stupid elf she shared that tiny room with. "If you think I've got some deep, dark secret, you're more delusional than King Sorrin."

"I think Rayn took an interest in you for a reason. I want to know what that reason is."

The princess shifted her hips uncomfortably. "We're kindred spirits. Two peas in a pod. We go together like trolls and body odor. That's all it is."

Pike snorted. "If you say so."

"You've really got it bad for her, don't you? Aww, you're just a big puppy deep down, huh? Too bad she's so far out of your league."

"*She's* out of *my* league? You know I was Evitankari's Council of War up until a few days ago, right? I was one of the most powerful men in the elven capital."

"Was?" Myrindi didn't know a ton about elven politics, but she had heard that those Council positions were usually held for life.

He chewed on the inside of his mouth, clearly debating how much to say. "Decided it wasn't worth it any more."

"So you quit because you couldn't handle it."

"Fuck you."

Myrindi cackled dramatically. "Bet you'd like to. Bag yourself a princess and all."

"I wouldn't touch you with a ten-foot pole if you were the last woman on earth. I'd be afraid to catch the stupid."

"Like you could get any dumber. You're just a sword on legs with a hard-on for my best friend."

"And you're just a walking baby maker the people in charge trot out for public appearances when they want to show just how in charge they really are," Pike snapped. "So which one of us really has it worse?"

"Fuck you."

Pike smiled. "That's the rub, isn't it? That's why you are the way you are. It's the only way you can hurt them. And for some fucked up reason, Rayn's encouraging it."

Myrindi rolled onto her right side, burying her face in the cushions and squeezing her eyes tight. "You will not speak to me again until Gol returns and it's time for us to leave."

"Whatever."

Dear Diary,

Pike has officially moved into the number three spot on the Royal List of People I Fucking Hate, right behind Sorrin and Gaptorix. He's narrowly edged out Dr. Neltsin and my second fiancé, Dremellon. Have I told you about that loser? No? Well, suffice to say my father took Rayn's demand that he find me a harmless husband far too seriously. Dremellon is the biggest pussy I've ever met. I'm not sure how he manages to stand up so straight without a having a spine to keep it all aligned. We were introduced approximately two months prior to my sixteenth birthday—the date on which Talvayan Crown Princesses traditionally marry the next king. Lard Ass obviously wasn't taking any chances. I'd kind of hoped he'd just forgotten about the whole marriage thing, but he'd really just been biding his time and attempting to reduce the chances of outside interference. As if. Rayn was coming to visit me every weekend at that point. "I promise you won't have to marry that troll," she reassured me the night before my second engagement party. She sat behind me, braiding my hair. "Play along for now so they don't try anything stupid."

I was scheduled to meet fiancé number two at a luncheon in the Emerald Hearth, a section of the Glittering Gardens famous for its lensing trees. These thick oak variants weave their boughs together to create a dense canopy that would block the sun out entirely if not for their semi-translucent leaves. Light passing through that canopy takes on a lime green tinge purported to stoke the feelings of young lovers. That, Diary, is your nature lesson for the day. I'm a woman of many surprising talents. And that green light makes me queasy, but whatever. Safe in the knowledge my BFF would rescue me from whatever horrible fate my father thought he could foist upon me, I slept in that morning and generally just didn't give a crap. I went light on the makeup, left my hair in the simple braid Rayn had done for me the night before, and chose a boring brown dress that made me look classy but not particularly interesting. No reason to get my wannabe husband's hopes up, right?

Father insisted on walking me through the Glittering Gardens. He hadn't spent more than ten minutes with me since Rayn and I ruined his victory meal with Sorrin. He'd somehow managed to get even bigger, which I'd never thought possible—stress eating, I assumed. He offered me his arm awkwardly and I took it, because sometimes a girl likes being escorted somewhere by her father even though he's a stupid prick she spends several hours a day mocking. Fuck you, Diary. Fro and Gaptorix fell into step behind us as we stepped out into the greenery. The part of the Glittering Gardens closest to the palace is a jungle, complete with impossibly tall trees, low-hanging vines, green leaves as big as my father, and narrow trails splitting off from the main brick pathway to private grottos and the occasional body of crystal clear water.

"Lovely day," he rumbled.

I just nodded. It was indeed a lovely day. I'd managed to make it through the morning without causing even a brief rain shower. The sun was shining, the birds were chirping, and a warm breeze wafted through the dense flora surrounding us. I was at peace, I guess. And why not? My new Tommy Hilfiger shades had arrived that morning and I'd gotten a positively delightful mani-pedi the day before.

"I think you'll like this one," Lard Ass said, his voice high with fake good humor. "He's a nice boy. Not a schemer like that Sorrin."

Interpretation: "he's completely harmless and won't give Rayn any reason to pummel me with lunch meat or whatever else is at hand." Gaptorix's burial via charcuterie is still one of my favorite things ever, if we're being honest. The big twit doesn't bathe all that regularly and he smelled like a bologna sandwich for a week.

Despite my father's attempts to make nice, I couldn't help myself. "Get anything good for me?"

Father blanched for a moment, his jaw agape, then he pursed his lips and answered excitedly. "More than I expected, actually. Five herds of cattle, a summer home on the Jersey Shore, and the Staff of Forinex."

Hamburgers, a hovel surrounded by spray-tanned bros, and a stick. Great.

Gaptorix snorted. "The Staff of Forinex is owned by the Rapgallivak clan," he growled. "You would marry your only daughter to those juice-drinking runt lovers?"

Lard Ass spun angrily on his heel, ready to tear into his uppity captain of the guard, then immediately backed down when he remembered Gaptorix could rip his nose off with one finger. "Such decisions are mine and mine alone, Gaptorix. You'd do well to remember that."

The hulking troll fumed for a moment, then relaxed and nodded his assent. I watched him for an extra second before turning back around, but he wouldn't meet my gaze. So Gaptorix didn't like my fiancé's family, huh? That didn't make a heck of a lot of sense. Although I didn't know the Rapgallivaks personally, that was an undeniably trollish name. The king typically takes care of his own species first and bestows upon them boons and benefits the other races are denied. That's part of the reason competition for the throne is so financially fierce. The Rapgallivaks' reputation must've really been in the shitter to make Gaptorix protest their rise to the throne.

Worse, all that meant I'd been promised to a fucking troll. Gross. No offense, Fro.

"What's this staff do?" I asked.

"It's one of Talvayne's most ancient and storied weapons," Lard Ass said proudly. "The Great Bhangoo himself wielded it in battle against Axzar when the Devourer lay siege to our city prior to unleashing the Rot."

"How'd that work out?"

"Our champion was felled in righteous battle."

"Not so well, then."

"The Great Bhangoo's valiant death makes his staff all the more important," he protested.

"Sure it does. I bet it's a really nice stick."

The path forked. A right turn would've taken us into the deciduous forest called Laurate's Wood, but we headed left into the Sea of Thorns, a broad field of roses that's actually a lot prettier than it sounds. Many portions of the Glittering Gardens have similar P.R. problems, such as Dildeaux's Cave, the Fluttering Fields of Fahkin Fahk, and Flatuland, to name a few. My people would've been much better off if we'd invented marketing before the humans thought of it. We'd had ample time. Not sure what the issue was.

Anyway, the Glittering Gardens are basically a smaller version of Talvayne. Each of the gardens is a different landscape, a self-contained climate with its own unique flora, fauna, and geological features. It takes three days to walk from one side to the other, and yet the entire thing is somehow enclosed within a half acre of land between the Palace of Light and the great wall that surrounds the Royal Estate. We fairy folk are big on our inconstancy. Can't have land that's the same for more than a mile or two or everyone loses their fucking minds. It's been that way forever, since the disparate fairy races first banded together to build a city of their own. None of them could agree on what the place should look like, so rather than working toward a consensus or just holding a vote they decided to make the land be whatever it needed to be. A complex spell tied the forces keeping the land diverse to the king himself—a predecessor, I suspect, to the magics linking the princess to the weather and the power that holds back the Rot.

"You know I've got a lot on my mind," Lard Ass rumbled as he paused to examine a large, offensively pink rose. "Talvayne doesn't hold *itself* together."

This again. Look, I don't doubt that being in charge of so many different types of people gets frustrating from time to time, but with my father that frustration was always just one big-ass excuse to not do something, ignore me, or fuck me over. I hadn't heard it in years, but to pull it out then and there— during our first real conversation since Rayn and I put him in his place—was, I imagine, rather like getting hit in the face with an entire table of lunch meat.

"I'm so sorry your life is hard because your evil doctor didn't get to scramble my brains," I snapped. I could feel both Fro and Gaptorix tensing up behind us.

Surprisingly, Father kept his composure. "You haven't exactly made things easy for me, Myrindi." He paused, suddenly looking wistful. "What exactly did I do to deserve the way you've always treated me?"

My own composure, however, didn't stand a chance. I crossed my arms and turned purple. My gills flared open angrily. "If you need me to explain to you how fucked up this whole system of royal succession is, you're even dumber than I thought."

He snorted. "We play the hand we're dealt, Myrindi. You should make the most of yours."

"Oh, I am. Just like Mother told me to."

"So that's where this came from." He paused to scratch his jowls, and then he smiled. "Let me tell you something: your mother was diagnosed with paranoid schizophrenia, chronic depression, and intense social anxiety disorder at age four. She spent the vast majority of her life on enough drugs to put Gaptorix in a coma. She had to be taken off that lovely cocktail while pregnant with you. Everything she may have told you was just the demented ravings of a certified lunatic with a severe chemical imbalance." He dragged those last three words out for dramatic effect, then squinted down at me as if daring me to try to refute his claims.

I just spun on my heel and stomped away. Lard Ass had gotten a metaphorical running start and drilled me right below the belt. The story had to be at least partly true; he wasn't stupid enough to waste his time lying to me in front of Fro, who'd watched over my mother the same way he watches over me. Still, he must've neglected a few pieces of information. There was no other explanation for the disconnect between what I knew of my mother's warm, calm, rational voice and what my father had just described. It didn't fit, but I didn't have the ammunition I needed to continue the argument—and I damn sure didn't want the big shithead to see me crying and know that he'd scored a victory. Fuck you, Diary. I mean, I'd built *everything* around what my mother had told me, so you can imagine how much of a shock the revelation of her deteriorating mental health was to my system. I suddenly felt a strange kinship to all those pop stars who get dumb haircuts and go off on five-year benders when they realize just how fake and manufactured they are.

My fists balled up tight and my face pinched, I power-walked toward the Emerald Hearth. I could hear Fro following a few feet behind me, but I didn't bother to turn around to see if my father and Gaptorix had kept up. If there was one thing I'd always be able to beat Lard Ass at, it was a foot race. Leaving him in my dust was the best retort I could muster, even though he'd have ample opportunity to gloat to himself as he crossed the Red Meadow, Fernbridge, and the Cloying Pines. I mean, fuck—what kind of halfwit named this shit?

I was about a dozen paces from our destination when a strong, rough hand snatched my wrist from behind and dragged me to a halt. "Princess, stop," Fro wheezed. He's a big tough guy, but he's built for short bursts of activity rather than extended, angry marches.

I jerked my arm out of his grasp. "Not now, Fro. I have to gouge my new fiancé's eye out with the jagged end of a broken champagne bottle so my father has to give his favorite new stick back." I fucking meant it, too.

This time his broad arm snaked out around my waist and he pulled me against his powerful chest. Before I could scream at him to fuck off, his free hand closed gently over my mouth and most of my face. I bit him, but his skin was so tough he didn't even notice. Fro's voice, typically deep and rough and not even remotely pretty, turned to soft silk. "It's true that your mother was not well. She struggled with a lot of demons her entire life. I spent my every waking moment with her, though, just like I have with you, and let me assure you of two things: her heart was always in the right place, and I never saw her as lucid as she was while carrying you."

And then he let me go, only to catch me again—gently this time—as I stumbled and almost fell. He released me once more, but I could feel his hand hovering near my elbow, ready if I needed help. I couldn't look back at him. I tossed my hair, set my shoulders confidently, and reminded myself that I'm the motherfucking princess.

"Get yourself together, Fro," I said haughtily. "We're about to meet the future king. A man of such refined culture and impressive breeding certainly won't stand for any interference from the help."

"Yes, Your Highness," he said. "We shouldn't leave the gentleman waiting." I could tell by the quiver in his voice that my carefully practiced irony—proof that he'd set me back on the right track—meant more to him than any other response could have. Fuck you, Diary, but on Fro's behalf this time.

"What crawled up Gaptorix's ass, by the way?"

"The captain of the guard is a bit of a...traditionalist. The Rapgallaviks are not. You'll understand when you see them."

Did I ever. I expected to hate my new fiancé on sight; I just didn't expect to hate him because he and his family looked like something out of a fifties sitcom. They burst out of their wicker chairs like a trio of dogs excited their master had come home, basically slapping me in the face with a torrent of wholesomeness as they waved and smiled and offered friendly greetings in voices far too high-pitched to come from any troll. The worst part? They *matched*. Father and son wore identical tweed suits tinged the color of week-old pea soup in the Emerald Hearth's green light. If you've never seen a troll in a bow tie, let me tell you something: it's really fucking hard not to laugh at a troll in a bow tie, especially when there are two of them.

"Hiiiiiiiyeeeeeeeeeee!" the woman shrieked at an octave that would've made a B-level pop diva jealous. The sound made no sense whatsoever coming out of her big ugly troll face. A demure dress made from the same material as the males' suits covered every inch of the mother's skin except her hands and face. "We're the Rapgallaviks! I'm Ravat, and this is Liptix, my husband." The old man nodded and took a puff from his pipe, clearly just waiting for his opportunity to regale us all with a spot of fatherly wisdom. Ravat motioned her son forward. "And this is Dremellon, our little bundle of joy!"

Her description couldn't have been more apt. I stood a good four inches taller than my husband-to-be. And you know that ecstatic look babies sometimes get when they shit themselves? Dremellon had that permanently etched into his face. He would've looked right at home in one of those little propellor hats.

"Where's the shaggy family dog?" I asked.

The joke went completely over their heads. "We left Rufus at home," Ravat replied. "That little scamp gets into oodles of hijinks when we bring him out in public!"

"I bet. Pardon me for a moment while I investigate the refreshments."

Blushing like he was asking a girl to dance for the first time, Dremellon took a step forward. "I'm happy to—"

"No."

I practically ran to the table of food and drink at the far end of the little grotto, Fro hot on my heels. I snapped up an unopened bottle of champagne, sent the cork spiraling off into the woods with a deft flick of my thumb, and greedily sucked down the bubbly spilling up over the top. "Just like Gaptorix said: juice-drinking runt-lovers," I whispered.

The corners of Fro's mouth twitched. Almost got him to smile. "You've heard of our practice of Al-Jahirix?"

I swished some champagne around in my cheek and then swallowed. "You trolls usually take children born small or sickly and leave them in the wild to fend for themselves. So what's up with shorty over there?"

"The Rapgallaviks are one of a growing number of clans who've done away with that tradition."

Glancing over my shoulder, I took a moment to examine my surroundings. The servants had once again done an excellent job creating a fantastic setting for an otherwise shitty occasion. Tables of food and drink ringed the outside edge of the Emerald Hearth, set tightly against the thick trees that defined the area. Garlands of pink and yellow roses dangled from the canopy like a loose spiderweb. The center had been converted into a brick patio that glowed faintly blue in the green light. There, five oversized wicker chairs and a trio of small tables provided a place for the Royal Family and our guests to get to know one another. The Rapgallaviks stood beside that furniture, smiling their big dumb smiles at me. I'd never seen trolls that frumpy. Each of the trio was badly out of shape, equipped with narrow shoulders and a heavy gut that betrayed a life of leisure. No wonder Gaptorix hated them. Perhaps he wasn't as bad a judge of character as I'd thought.

At this point you probably think I'm an asshole. To a certain extent, you're probably right. But let me fill you in on a little something: the Rapgallaviks may seem to be a perfectly nice family with impeccable etiquette and an unbreakable moral code, but a *real* perfectly nice family with impeccable etiquette and an unbreakable moral code would never, ever buy a princess for their son. Now there's some wholesome fatherly wisdom for ya, Diary. I hope you're taking notes. Wait. Of course you are. Shit.

Gaptorix's voice boomed from the other side of the grotto. "May I announce his Royal Highness, King Luminad XIII, Defender of the Realm, Keeper of the Light, and Bringer of Justice!"

"...and Scourge of Pies Everywhere," I added under my breath.

The Rapgallaviks all knelt. Father toddled into the Emerald Hearth, his best plastic smile spread wide across his face. "Rise, my friends, rise!" he shouted merrily. "Family need not kneel to one another!"

Gaptorix had taken up a position beside the entrance. I thought I saw a burst of smoke explode from each of his ears. Although Rayn had promised to rescue me before the wedding, I couldn't help wishing I'd get to see King Dremellon try to order the big guy around—at least for an afternoon.

Father went to Ravat first and wrapped his arms around her in a big, fleshy hug. His hand drifted down to her right ass cheek and gave it a quick squeeze. Ravat's smile brightened in response. I should've known. The public enjoyed the narrative claiming the Talvayan kings suffered their reigns in resolute celibacy out of respect for their departed queens, but those of us who lived in the palace all knew there was no bigger pile of bullshit in the entire realm. My father, at least, had been one of the better kings when it came to keeping his business secret. Seeing it so blatantly—and immediately understanding my own role in his little tryst—made me uncomfortable, like if one of the servants had suggested I wear plaid. I mean, was Lard Ass even physically attracted to her? My mother had been a frail little thing about the size of Ravat's left toenail, but I guess that wasn't much to go on given the way royal marriages are arranged. So did Father want Dremellon's mother, or was banging her just another of his stupid superiority games? I don't know, but I've got five bucks that says Ravat's husband knew about and condoned the whole arrangement as part of the whole marriage deal.

Lard Ass moved on to shake Liptix's hand, then Dremellon's. Platitudes and niceties were exchanged. I drained my bottle of champagne and opened another one. Rayn had told me to sit tight, to go with the flow, to refrain from rocking the boat, to "not be myself" as Pike so eloquently put it. No one knows me better than my bestie, but she badly underestimated both my desire to make my father's life miserable and his innate ability to piss me off. I couldn't shake the impression that this entire day was basically just one long victory lap for him. I'm sure he would've asked the Rapgallaviks to shower him in champagne right then and there if it had been socially acceptable.

I couldn't let the big jackass win. Not after what he'd pulled on the way over here. I glanced back across the grotto at Gaptorix, who glowered at the Rapgallaviks as if trying to decide which one of them to eat first. "There's my bitch," I muttered evilly before I moved to join my father and our guests.

Father saw me coming and grinned as if he'd just eaten a whole truckload of shit. "And here's the woman of the hour! Myrindi, say hello."

"Hello," I muttered demurely, feigning defeat. "A pleasure to meet you all."

Lard Ass was too blinded by what he thought was a permanent victory to realize I was up to something. "The light of my life, this one," he rumbled merrily. "A model princess to which all future princesses can look to as an example."

"Thank you, Father," I croaked. I looked to Ravat. "You've got a lovely family, ma'am."

The troll beamed like she'd just won an Academy Award. She reached out her meaty arms and pulled her two men in close. It was like looking at the cheesy album cover of a terrible family band. "You're kind to say so, Your Highness, and may I say that we all look forward to making you a big part of our lives."

"I'd like that," I said, trying to force myself to blush. I don't think it worked. "I've heard the Rapgallaviks are a noble people, true leaders when it comes to redefining what it means to be a troll in modern times." Gaptorix's snort made my heart flutter.

"We try, Your Highness," Liptix replied, taking a quick puff on his pipe. "We may look like brutes, but that's no excuse to act like monsters. We have hopes, dreams, and emotions just like everyone else. It's high time we embraced them all without relying on violence as our kind has in the past."

Right. Better to pimp out your wife to buy your son a princess than stand up and prove your worth. I somehow managed to bite my tongue on that one. "A wise and brave philosophy, sir, and one that seems to have served your son well."

Ravat squeezed Dremellon's shoulder protectively. "Al-Jahirix has extinguished far too many bright little lights," she said sadly. "Allowing such a barbaric tradition to darken our lives was never an option."

"Luckily for me," I replied, "or I wouldn't have such a handsome fiancé."

That drew a round of polite laughter from Father and the Rapgallaviks. Dremellon blushed and studied his shoes. I swear I could hear Gaptorix's blood pounding through his 'roided-out veins.

"Well, I for one cannot wait to dive into that lovely brunch over there," Father said. "Liptix, Ravat...shall we give our two young lovebirds a few minutes to get to know each other?"

"A capital idea, Your Highness!" Liptix replied.

As the three adults stepped away to join Fro at the refreshment table, Ravat turned back to face Dremellon and me. "You two behave yourselves!" she chirped, wagging her finger. "Save a few things for the wedding night!"

"Your son's virtue is safe with me!" I replied. I considered the rest of him, however, fair game.

Dremellon looked up at me with his beady eyes wide and his thick lips quivering. I'm pretty sure he would've been crying if trolls had tear ducts. "It's nice to finally meet you," he sputtered pathetically.

"You too, Dremellon. Do you think I'll make a good wife?"

"Y-y-yes!" His eyes kept flicking between me and his parents. He obviously couldn't handle being separated from them.

"And I think you'll make a great husband." My mind raced. I needed to trick him into doing something ridiculously un-troll-like and embarrassing. I didn't think that would take much prodding, but I still wasn't quite sure how to go about it.

Luckily, Dremellon came to my rescue. "I wrote you a p-p-poem."

Perfect. "That's so sweet. Will you read it to me?"

He nodded like an excited puppy and yanked a square of notebook paper out of his back pocket. "I've been working on this since I first heard we were going to get married," he explained as his nubby little fingers worked to unfold the page. "I write in secret after Mom and Dad put me to bed. Please d-d-don't tell."

"I won't. Promise. What time is bedtime?"

"Eight o'clock sharp!"

"And how old are you?"

"Twenty-five!"

That's even better when you know it's trollish tradition to consider a child grown and ready to face the world at age ten. "Well, when we're husband and wife, you can stay up as late as you want, as long as you keep me entertained," I said happily. I could tell from the blank look in his eyes that he completely missed what I was implying. "Read me that poem."

"Okay." He paused for a moment to clear his throat and properly position the ratty piece of paper on which he'd scribbled his masterpiece, and then he began to read:

Roses are red,
Your skin is blue.
When I'm the king
You'll be my boo.

I love my mommy
And my daddy too
Sometimes I wet the bed
But I'll try not to hit you.

That was a joke
I haven't had an accident in six months
But I'll tell you right now
I really love you a bunch.

I'll be the king
And you'll be the queen.
We'll rule Talvayne
As an unstoppable team.

Then when you die
I'll miss you lots
But I'll take care of our daughter
And wipe off her snots.

I started quivering with laughter after the second line. I'm still not sure how I managed to keep a straight face. That part about my unavoidable death during childbirth was a bit of a low blow, but otherwise the entire thing was high comedy. I wanted to put little Dremellon under my arm, carry him back to my chambers, and make him perform the poem again in front of Rayn so we could spend the rest of the evening imitating and making fun of the little twat.

"Very good, Dremellon," I said, my voice cracking under the concentrated force of will it took to refrain from rolling around on the ground while laughing my ass off. I made a show of searching the area for someone's assistance. "I don't know much about trollish poetry, however. Hey...Gaptorix! What did you think?"

The big captain of the guard crossed his arms and growled, a sound like he'd swallowed a running chainsaw. "A real troll writes of smiting his enemies, taking their property as his own, and reveling in the lamentations of their women and children. We do *not* write of love, happiness, or..." He shuddered. "...snots. I do not know which is the worse abomination: that poem or its lettuce-eating, blanket-loving poet."

Dremellon visibly deflated. "I'm sorry," he croaked.

That drew the attention of my fiancé's father. Liptix stormed over from the refreshments table to confront his son's tormentor. "Now, see here, Gaptorix! That sort of old-fashioned malarkey is just as extinct as the dodo. We live in an era of peace and harmony, mister, and your brutal traditions have no place in the world we've created!"

Gaptorix snorted. I swear I saw flames burst from his nostrils. "You and your freakish spawn diminish our great race. Tradition has made us strong. Ignoring it will be our undoing. That runt should've been abandoned in a place where his inferior genes can never taint our future."

Liptix glowered at the captain of the guard and took a long drag from his pipe. He blew a steady stream of smoke right into Gaptorix's face. "That is your future king you're insulting."

The bigger troll didn't even blink. He snatched Liptix's pipe, crushed it between his fingers, and tossed it aside. "I will serve King Luminad XIII until the day of his daughter's wedding, but I will *never* swear fealty to your son." He turned on his heel and stomped out of the Emerald Hearth, leaving the rest of us in stunned silence.

And that's how I inadvertently planted the seeds for the military coup that took my father's life. That part probably won't wind up in the history books.

— CHAPTER EIGHT —

About half an hour after sundown, Gol returned to the loading dock's office with a pair of brown cloaks. Had either Pike or Myrindi known anything about sand nymph physiology, they would've known that the wildly swirling grains in her cheeks indicated emotional distress. Myrindi assumed Gol had some sort of skin disease and Pike thought he was hallucinating because he'd eaten something spoiled.

"Ready to go?" the apprentice archivist asked.

Myrindi spun off the couch and popped to her feet. Pike stood and reached for his armor.

"Leave that," Gol said. "Makes you too easy to spot, even at night. And it won't fit under this." She offered the big elf the larger of the two cloaks she carried.

Pike frowned at her as if she'd just told him the sky was purple. "So go find me a bigger disguise. You have any idea how much I paid for this?"

"Yeah!" Myrindi chimed in playfully. "Do you *even know* how many empty cans and bottles he had to steal from the neighbors' trash so he could afford that shit?"

"Fuck you," Pike growled.

"Do you load them all up in a shopping cart or just drag a bag around behind you?"

Gol sighed and rolled her eyes. She'd done that a lot in the short time she'd known Pike and Myrindi. "Your armor will be safe here," she said diplomatically. "I'll sneak it out separately—later. Lep and Chas are dealing with the trolls in the gatehouse. We can't leave them waiting."

That got the big elf moving. It was the first news he'd heard of his companions since they'd been separated earlier in the day. "Let's get this show on the fucking road, then," he said as he slipped past Gol, snatched the larger cloak out of her hand, and stomped out of the office.

The short sand nymph ignored him and turned her attention to Myrindi. "Your Highness...we have to cross fifty feet of courtyard to reach the gate. It's not pretty out there."

"I know," the princess replied as she shrugged into her cloak. "Groundskeepers never cut the damn grass evenly. Can't trust those gnomes to do even simple tasks."

Gol smiled sadly and shook her head. "That's not it, Your Highness." She hesitated as if speaking the words would burn her mouth. "The courtyard's full of corpses. Sorrin's dumping bodies out there."

"That stupid fucking stump dares to kill *my* people?" Myrindi spat. "Who?"

"I don't know. I didn't want to look very closely." She reached into her pocket and produced an empty glass jar with a silver lid. "If you'd rather not see that sort of thing, Your Highness, I'd be happy to carry you."

Myrindi balled her fists and shook her head angrily. "I can handle it. Dealing with such atrocities is all part of being princess." She shrugged into her cloak and flipped the hood up over her head emphatically.

Gol nodded and set the jar down on the nearby desk. "Yes, Your Highness. We should hurry."

The loading dock outside the office was a boring cube of splotched concrete just big enough to admit a large van or carriage. Double doors on either side led back into the palace. A large garage door opposite the office opened up into the courtyard. Pike, now concealed in his cloak, stood at the chain used to raise and lower it.

"Ready?" he asked.

The two women nodded.

"I'm only going to raise it far enough for everybody to crawl underneath. No need to make anyone suspicious of a wide open door. Gol's first, the princess is second, and I'll take up the rear. If anyone comes for us, it'll be from the palace. Stay in the grass to the side of the driveway to hide the sound of your footsteps. Keep your heads down and your butts moving."

Pike didn't wait for an acknowledgment. He raised the door a few feet with one mighty yank of the chain. Thankfully, the loading dock's staff took good care of the mechanisms involved and the noise was kept to a minimum. Gol dropped to the floor and rolled out into the courtyard beyond. Myrindi gently got onto her hands and knees, eyed the gap warily, then glowered up at Pike. "You'd better not stare at my ass the whole way."

"Don't worry, your Royal Flatness," he replied without missing a beat. "You don't have an ass for me to stare at."

Myrindi spat on the toes of Pike's nearest boot and scrambled under the door. Gol reached down and helped her to her feet. It was a dark, cloudy evening, but light streaming out from windows in the palace made it easy to see. The outer wall and the nearest gate were a straight shot across a paved driveway, just as Gol had described. The land around them, however, looked like a war zone. Bodies littered the grass, many surrounded by pools of blood in various states of drying. Most were within fifteen feet of the palace itself.

Pike crawled out into the courtyard and quickly surveyed the scene. "Fucker's probably throwing them out the windows."

Myrindi shifted uncomfortably. She pointed at a dead gnoll to her left. "That's Shit-for-Brains. Over there's Curbside Fellatio. That's Litter Box. I know all of them—well, not by name because they're all assholes, but I *know* all of these people."

"The hell are you talking about?" Pike asked.

"The Conclave. Sorrin's killing all the kings."

The big elf scratched his chin. "Ballsy. We'll worry about it later. Go."

They took off at a run in the order Pike had dictated: Gol first, Myrindi second, and Pike himself bringing up the rear. Myrindi glanced over her shoulder from time to time to make sure Pike's eyes weren't somewhere they shouldn't have been, but he was more interested in making sure they weren't about to get flanked. They reached the gatehouse without incident and gathered around the narrow door beside the closed portcullis.

Gol tested the handle gently; it didn't budge. "Now what?" she whispered.

Pike shrugged and knocked on the door.

"Password?" asked a familiar voice from within.

"Go fuck yourself," Pike replied.

"Password accepted." Lep opened the door and waved them all inside. In the room behind him, Chastity and Fro looted equipment from a pair of dead trolls. They all wore cloaks similar to what Gol had brought Pike and Myrindi. Chastity had a few bandages on her right arm and Lep sported a killer black eye.

"Princess!" Fro hissed as Myrindi entered the narrow space. "It is good to see you."

Lep quickly shut the door behind them. "We had a chance to talk with a few of the servants. Sorrin's working quickly to consolidate his power. He's called in the reserve guards and secured all the armories around Talvayne."

"There's a bunch of dead kings on the lawn, too," Pike replied. "Fucker's not messing around."

"His claim to the throne is tenuous at best," Fro said. "Marrying Myrindi would secure that hold, but opposition from the Conclave would make his rule...difficult."

"Whatever," the princess said. "Let's just make sure he can't marry Myrindi. She wouldn't be very happy with that."

Lep grunted. "Gol, what's our next stop?"

The sand nymph smiled up at him. "My house."

Dear Diary,

Gol, being a sand nymph and all, lives in a hole in half an acre of desert about thirty minutes from the palace. It's easy to miss; there's a giant storm cloud full of wisps on one side, an arctic tundra on the other, and the entrance to her house is hidden in the back side of a boring sand dune that looks just like all the other boring sand dunes in that particular plot. It's nice enough on the inside, I guess: hardwood floors, crisp white walls and ceilings, a few post-modern sculptures that look vaguely sexual and feminine. There's definitely room for improvement, though. I promised Gol I'd hook her up with my decorator once this is all over. Her family lives there too: mother, father, and a super cute older brother. Dude's like something right out of a young adult movie with vampires and werewolves and such. I haven't had the chance to talk to him—yet—but he winked at me as his mother whisked me away to the master bathroom so I could freshen up. Their shower's a little small, but right now it's definitely the best fucking shower ever. I'd never thought that people made of sand would need to bathe. You learn something new every day.

Gaptorix's men are all over Talvayne, patrolling in seemingly random intervals. Lep thinks we should try to get a better handle on things before proceeding too far. We crossed the city slowly and carefully, sticking to the shadows and cutting across pieces of land that offered the best cover, but we still almost got caught three or four times. I'd prefer to get the hell out of Talvayne as quickly as possible, but Fro agrees with Lep's cautious approach. That's good enough for me.

I've got a lot on my mind, Diary. Too much. Father's dead. Twat Face Jr. and Gaptorix are in control of the palace and the city. My social calendar's all messed up. I still can't figure out why my bestie gave me a pinwheel. I don't want to think about any of it because it makes my head hurt, so I'm going to tell you the story of the night before my wedding instead. You know, for posterity.

Rayn said she would come for me; she just didn't say exactly when. Midnight hit and I was justifiably a bit concerned. I mean, I trust my bestie implicitly, but it wasn't like she was late for girls' night or a trip to the spa. If she didn't show, I was going to have to marry Dremellon. I hadn't bothered to whip up a backup plan. I ordered the servants to keep a pot of coffee warm and stayed up watching my old Britney DVDs and biting my nails and fighting off my mounting exhaustion.

Fro sat on the sofa with me. He'd never done that before. "You should get some sleep," he told me more than a few times. "Tomorrow will go smoother if you're well rested." He thought I was just trying to delay the inevitable; he had no clue I was waiting for salvation.

My bestie finally showed up around two in the morning. She just sort of melted into my parlor through one of the windows on the west side. Rayn's got a weird obsession with making an entrance. I've seen her pop out of closets, fall from the sky, step through mirrors, slither out of lampshades, and ooze out of televisions. Once she even burst out of Fro's back pocket. She always looks way too pleased immediately after the fact. I'm pretty sure she just does it to keep herself amused.

As usual, Fro's eyes closed and his head dipped as soon as Rayn entered the room. She's my friend, but sometimes I can't help being a little freaked out by the things she can do. I'm not sure anyone could stop her if she really wanted something.

She paused by the window to fix a few strands of long black hair that had come out of place. "Ready to ditch this joint?" she asked mischievously.

"You'd better fuckin' believe it," I replied as I slipped off my sofa. I'd worn a thin white shift and matching ballet flats for the occasion. Rayn had asked me not to wear anything too princess-y, but that was no reason to look like I'd purchased my outfit at some shitty department store. Simple's all the rage in Paris right now.

"None of this is going to make any sense," Rayn said, almost apologetically.

"With you, I didn't really expect it to."

"It's going to make even less sense than usual."

"Less sense than going through with a wedding to a stunted runt whose family paid mine for the privilege?"

"Definitely not. Just remember that everything that's about to happen is all part of the plan, and sometimes you have to take three steps backward before you can take even a single step forward."

"Are you feeling all right? Eat something that disagreed with you? Let's go already!"

Rayn rubbed her palms together and a rubber ducky suddenly appeared in her left hand. She put it down on the end table beside the sofa. It squeaked when she gave its plastic body a squeeze. "This is a transpoint encoded to a single destination. It will get you where you need to go."

I hesitated. "You're not coming with me?"

She shook her head. "I'll meet you there. Things to do, people to see, plots to advance. Busy as a bee."

"So you're just going to leave me with a bunch of strangers? I thought it was going to be you and me against the world, Rayn, like Thelma and Louise with better style and more magic."

"To be honest, you won't even know I'm not there. You won't arrive until I'm at your destination. You're going to be trapped in the transpoint network until I let you out."

Normally, all transpoints in the world are connected to each other. Travel from one to another involves merely touching one and picturing your destination. It's how Talvayne's inhabitants get past the Rot to travel and trade with the outside world. Rayn had procured—or perhaps created—a bootleg, stripped-down model. I glared at her. "How fucking long?"

She shrugged. "A day, maybe two. I need some time to make sure all my ducks are in a row." She squeezed the transpoint again. "You won't notice the time pass."

"Is that even safe? I mean, what good is running away through this scram-ass transpoint if I end up with one of my arms growing out of my face?"

"I wouldn't ask you to do it if it wasn't safe."

"Tried it yourself?"

"Tested with a gnome."

"No you didn't."

"No, I didn't. But I guarantee any side effects it may cause won't be worse than marrying Dremellon."

I snatched up the rubber ducky. "How does it work?"

"You have to say the magic words."

"And those are?"

"'Get me the fuck out of here.'"

"Apropos."

"When I let you out, you'll be met by a man named Demson or one of his subordinates. He's going to think he bought you."

I did a double-take. "So how is this plan different from my pending nuptials?"

"Don't worry: I'm totally using him for my own ends. Got him wrapped around my finger so tightly he can't even fart without my permission. He thinks he's arranged your kidnapping through a group of radical socialist wisps dissatisfied with the Talvayan monarchy. He does not know of my involvement in this, or of my friendship with you—and I would prefer to keep it that way."

I pantomimed zipping my lips.

"Good. I'll arrive soon after with an associate of mine I'm looking to plant in a particular situation. Shit will spiral out of control from there, but don't worry: everything that happens is all just part of the plan."

We high-fived. I know what you're thinking, Diary: I'm too gullible, too willing to trust someone dangerous and mysterious who obviously has her own secret agenda. I disagree. Rayn's done more for me than any other person in my life. I was happy to go along with her, even though I knew she was at least partly using me for something shady. I didn't dare ask what. She was my *only* ticket out, you know? And even though everything's gone kind of sideways, I don't regret allying with her. Besides, what the hell else was I supposed to do? Just lie down and accept my inevitable death-by-bearing-some-goober's-child? That ain't me.

"Anything left to take care of before you go?"

I patted Fro on the shoulder. I knew he wouldn't be happy when he woke up, but I had decided that bringing him into my confidence was too big a risk. Even leaving a note would be revealing too much. Sorry, Fro.

I gave the rubber ducky a playful squeeze. "Get me the fuck out of here."

Blue light flared around me and electricity raced through my body. The sensation was unpleasant, but it was over before I had time to bitch about it. I found myself standing beside a well-appointed bar, a bottle of expensive vodka in my hand where I'd previously held the rubber ducky. The room around me was super nice. It was tiny—a square room about twenty feet on each side—but extremely classy. Nearly every surface was granite, nearly every fixture gold. A trio of secluded booths with optional privacy curtains lined the wall behind me. I quickly scanned the liquor collection above the bar and couldn't have been more impressed with the owner's taste. Rayn's bootleg transpoint had deposited me right in the VIP— exactly where I belonged. A wave of nausea washed over me as my body adjusted to the transition, but I fought it down. "Funky," I muttered.

"Welcome to Beijing. My name is Demson," said the old business douche beside me. I know a self-important twit when I see one, and this guy was definitely a grade A cunt wagon. Gray pinstriped suit, light blue shirt with a dark blue tie, glittering gold watch and cufflinks—and none of it fit properly. The mess of wrinkles criss-crossing his face betrayed both his age and his aversion to moisturizer. A bright red eye burned brightly from the middle of his forehead, set above and between his otherwise normal brown peepers. Otherwise, he appeared to be human—which meant he was a demon, a man twisted by his evil deeds into a raging bag of villainy and general dickishness. Not exactly the sort of person I'd expected Rayn to drop me next to, but I rolled with it.

"How's it hangin'?" I slurred, still a little unsettled from the transition.

He didn't miss a beat. "Same shit, different day. Elves have been knocking my towers down. I'm massing my forces to hit their capital, but I wanted to make sure I held a powerful piece of leverage over their strongest ally before I make my move."

"So that's why you bought a princess!"

Demson smiled. "You, my dear, are just as smart as you are beautiful."

"Aww! I bet you say that to all the girls you kidnap!"

His grin faded slightly. "You're awfully chipper for someone wrenched from her home against her will."

He had a point. I decided a version of the truth with generic thugs in Rayn's place would be best. "Did you hear about that fucking dork I was supposed to marry? You have no clue how big of a favor you did my uterus."

His big red eye narrowed. "You understand that you are absolutely a prisoner here and that my manners are in no way indicative of any good will toward your person or your anatomy, correct?"

I nodded enthusiastically and decided to double down. "You're coming through loud and clear, oh captor of mine. Just trust me when I say that there are most assuredly certain fates far worse than conversing with a well-spoken gentleman in a *swank* club. One of those things is being sold to a greasy troll like you're some sort of accessory. Besides, you seem like a mover and a shaker, and I'm royalty with lots of influence and a serious problem. Let's do business, doll face."

"What sort of business?"

"I imagine you're planning to hold me here until you're done playing angel of vengeance with your elven enemies, and then you're going to ransom me back to Talvayne, yes?"

He nodded.

"Well, who better to have on your side than the *Queen* of Talvayne? Especially if she helps you install a handsome, dashing, socially acceptable and politically malleable *king* as part of your ransom demands? Just think: next time some asshole knocks down a few of your towers, you won't have to kidnap a princess to keep Talvayne out of the fray—you'll have the option of asking us nicely instead."

Demson didn't speak for a few seconds as he digested my suggestion. I couldn't tell if he was going to agree or slap me in the face. Maybe I'd spoken too quickly for him to keep up.

Finally, he broke into an even wider smile. "I like the way you think."

I shrugged. "Most intelligent, rational individuals do." Rayn ain't the only one who can play this fucking game. I still trusted her to come through for me, but having a plan of my own certainly wouldn't hurt, now would it?

The old demon stood, his joints audibly cracking. "Will you join me for dinner, Your Highness? I've several associates who would *love* to meet Talvayan royalty."

"Certainly, darling," I replied smoothly. "What better way to seal our new friendship?"

The double doors on the other side of the room blew open and collided with the brass stops on the wall with a loud bang. Rayn slithered in like she owned the place, her dark eyes raking the bar and the surrounding booths like they were made of cheap garbage. A blond woman with antlers sticking out of her head trailed her cautiously—another demon, most likely, but one that hadn't been following the evil douche path for nearly as long as Demson and thus wasn't so...gross. Like Chastity, I assume.

"Demsooooooooon!" Rayn cooed in her best teenaged girl voice. "You aren't cheating on me with that little blue harlot, are you?" She favored me with a quick wink but otherwise gave no indication of recognizing me.

Demson laughed melodramatically. "I'd like to introduce you to my newest acquaintance: Myrindi, Crown Princess of Talvayne."

Rayn shook my hand gently. "Charmed. I've heard so many good things."

"Lies. All of them."

"As are all the bad things they say about me. I'm the Witch."

I knew of Rayn's alias, of course, but I'd rarely heard her use it herself. I'd never thought it a good fit for the woman I knew as my bestie, but somehow it fit the darker version of her that stood before me right then. She'd put on an extra layer of asshole for the occasion.

"Who's your friend?" I asked. The other woman had taken a seat at the far end of the bar and opened a thick old book.

"The nerd's name is Talora," Rayn replied. "She's got her uses, but she's kind of a bitch."

Without bothering to look up from her book, Talora scratched her eye with her middle finger.

"See what I mean?" Rayn turned back to Demson. "What's for dinner?"

"Expensive food and liquor."

She feigned indignity. "You don't feed me nearly that well when we aren't hosting a princess!"

"Royalty demands more than pepperoni pizza and root beer, my dear."

"Damn straight," I replied. Rayn and I traded a quick look. Her eyes glittered mischievously.

Dinner was served on the roof. Turns out I'd been dumped into a night club in downtown Beijing named Iki, one of the many properties owned by Demson's company: the notorious Tallisker. What little I'd heard of the shady multinational conglomerate wasn't good. Mostly they focused their bitch-ass-ness on humanity. Anywhere there was war, famine, genocide, slavery, or other such unnecessary fuckery, Tallisker was right there in the middle of it, turning a handsome profit and feeding their insatiable appetite for evil. They sold guns and drugs, funded oppressive regimes, and manipulated huge chunks of the global economy thanks to a monstrous portfolio of stocks, bonds, assets, and agents more complicated and twisted than the cast of your average dating show. Demson and his ilk were the worst of the worst, and Rayn was fucking with them because *of course* she was. In the back of my mind, I couldn't help worrying that she'd dragged me into the middle of something she wouldn't be able to pull me out of.

Anyway, the meal itself was pleasant enough despite the impressive array of douche nozzles in attendance. When you come right down to it, the whole affair wasn't all that different from the various functions my father had shuffled me off to with the Conclave of Kings. I was pretty used to being surrounded by pompous wind bags doing their damnedest to both impress and undercut each other. I'd given each of Demson's demon pals fun nicknames within five minutes of sitting down, but I can't remember any of them now. The whole scene isn't really worth talking about, with one exception: the view was unlike anything I've ever seen. Talvayne's a diverse, densely packed city, but it's got nothing that looks even remotely like Beijing's skyscrapers. All that metal and glass in one place was just as intimidating as it was beautiful. A layer of hazy smog gave it all an ethereal, dirty quality. The city seemed to go on forever and ever and ever, like a Kanye acceptance speech or dessert with my father. I couldn't decide if I liked it. I definitely didn't enjoy the taste of whatever shit the surrounding human population had pumped into the air. Made my gills itch. That's one of the main reasons I mostly abstained from the banal conversation ricocheting sluggishly back and forth across the table.

Do I sound less than enthusiastic about this whole situation? Sorry. This part's hard for me, and it's getting harder the more I think about it. I always imagined my escape from Talvayne would lend itself a lot better to the inevitable movie adaptation. I'll make sure my ghostwriter takes plenty of liberties with this particular scene. It was probably pretty exciting for everyone else involved—Talora got to be handcuffed to a princess (I guess they wanted us to watch each other or something) and Demson's precious nightclub was sacked by an elven commando squad— but I can't help looking back on it as a bit of a letdown for the relative lack of snappy dialogue and hot outfits.

So yeah, about that commando squad. The elves of Evitankari came to rescue me not long after dinner. A group atop a nearby roof caused a magic thunderstorm on the main club floors to empty the place out while their buddies snuck in through the back door—and right into an array of explosives Demson had set up as a trap. Blowing up part of your own club might not seem like the smartest idea, but I guess it's something most intruders wouldn't see coming.

Talora and I ditched that place quicker than I got rid of last year's spring collection. We'd been stashed in a VIP room by ourselves, still handcuffed to each other. Rayn had made it very clear she wanted us out at the first opportunity. Beijing was just a short layover on my journey, a smokescreen designed to place the blame for my disappearance plainly on the shoulders of Demson and the Tallisker dorks. Rayn hadn't explained it as such—she'd been annoyingly vague about her plan—but there was no other explanation. Well, there was, but the idea that she hadn't thought everything through in the most minute detail wasn't a possibility I was willing to acknowledge.

The street outside Iki was a roiling storm of shit. Various demons of all twisted shapes and nonsensical sizes squared off with three elven agents: two gunmen and one sorceress, all wearing classy black commando fatigues and body armor. Paramilitary chic hasn't caught on yet, but I'm a fan. Judging from the mess of bodies on the ground, the demons weren't doing so well. Talora didn't give me a chance to determine the exact score. She almost tore my arm off when she yanked me down the street. I ran as hard as I could, dead set on keeping up. Heavy boots clacking on the pavement betrayed the lone elf fucker that decided to follow.

Rayn had given us very specific directions: two rights and then our second left to the backup getaway car in front of the noodle joint. Talora decided not to use them. She took a left down a narrow side street instead. I didn't protest; I was chained to her arm, after all, and she had a good forty or fifty pounds on me. Getting away from whoever was following us seemed more important. Guess I could've liquified if I'd really wanted to, but that street was gross.

Turns out Talora's sense of direction is worse than her taste in makeup. Seriously, her blush and mascara were whack. She led us straight into a dead end. That alley smelled like shit. I tried to stand on my tip-toes to minimize contact with whatever microscopic parasites had infested the sticky concrete. Anyone who thinks the Rot is the most disgusting thing on the planet has obviously never been to Beijing.

Our pursuer, of course, caught us. Tall and lean and kind of handsome in a dorky middle-aged way, he looked more like someone's awkward, doddering dad than a bad-ass commando, even in that hot uniform. He carried a flashlight in one hand and a beat-up old shotgun in the other. I got the distinct impression he'd never done this sort of thing before. To be honest, Diary, it was pretty insulting. I mean, Evitankari thought it was rescuing an innocent princess from the clutches of evil, and this goof was the best they could send? Seriously. Must be a shortage of hunky warrior types in elf-land these days. Maybe that's why Lep and Pike struck out on their own.

"Come peacefully," he wheezed, "and I'll make sure you get the help you need."

I wanted to tell him I didn't need any fucking help from some busybody on a power trip, but Talora cut in front of me. "I have a message for Pentari Roger Brooks."

"Do you mean Pintiri Roger Brooks?" he asked in a tone that suggested he may have just made a mess in his commando pants.

Talora faked a laugh, obviously annoyed. "Whatever. It's in the top of my dress."

"I'm Pintiri Roger Brooks," the man said, because of course he was. "Hand me the message."

I began to feel a bit peeved. This was supposed to be *my* escape from Talvayne, damn it, and Rayn had twisted it into whatever *the hell* was going on between her lackey and this dork. I felt like...like *bait*. I am *not* bait. Did you get all those italics, Diary? Good. Wish I could actually see you to make sure. Lots of things are pissing me off that require appropriate emphasis. Remind me to get you back from Fro.

Talora pulled a glittery purple envelope out of her dress and offered it to Roger. He motioned to me with his flashlight. "Open it and hold it up so I can see it."

Whatever. I held the sweat-stained envelope at arm's length and tore it open gingerly. The white card inside was made of cheap stock, flimsy and poorly creased. "Missing you" ran across the top of the card in cartoony block letters above a sad-looking teddy bear. I flipped it open and held it up so Roger could read it. The man's eyes flicked across it quickly, then his jaw dropped and his face turned white. He just stood there in a catatonic state like he'd run out of batteries or been petrified by some rune inscribed in the card's interior. I was about to wave a few fingers in front of his face when he suddenly shoved his flashlight into my free hand.

"Hold this."

Roger stomped past me with murder in his eyes. Flames burst to life in Talora's hands as she prepared to defend herself. She never got the chance. Roger drilled her in the face with a handful of silver dust that exploded around her like a cloud of glitter. One breath of that stuff was all it took. Talora's eyes rolled back in her head, her body went slack, and she collapsed to the nasty street. We were still handcuffed together, so guess what happened? Luckily I mostly landed on her midsection, but my left hand touched the concrete. I haven't eaten with it since.

"The fuck was that about?" I snapped at my would-be rescuer.

He knelt to scoop up the greeting card and the flashlight, both of which I'd dropped while being dragged down by a basic bitch-shaped anchor. "It's personal," he grunted. "Are you Princess Myrindi?"

I stood and brushed myself off. Talora's arm hung limply from the cuff at my wrist. "No, I'm not."

Roger squinted at me, clearly confused. "Yes, you are."

"Fine. You got me."

"I'm here to rescue you."

"From what?"

He glanced nervously around the alley. When he turned his head, I noticed his ears lacked the usual pointy elven tips. "This," he stammered. "Those people back there."

"You're human," I gasped. This rescue attempt was even crappier than I'd first suspected.

"I'm the Pintiri," he said, as if that explained it all.

The Pintiri is Evitankari's champion, the elves' top cop, the meddling jerk they send when they want to mess with something serious. He's supposed to be the best of their best. So how the hell did this loser get the job? That said loser was human made the whole thing even more confusing. Those poor bastards aren't even supposed to *know* about the rest of us. Either something had gone horribly wrong with the elves' selection process, or their best just ain't what it used to be. "How in the fuck did that happen?"

Roger shrugged. "I'm not really sure."

"Great." I rattled the handcuff around my wrist. "Say...how about you get me out of these things so I can get the heck out of here?"

He took a step forward and shined his flashlight at the problem. "Uh..."

I sighed and shook my head. "Useless. That body armor looks waterproof. Take it off and put it on the street so I've got something relatively clean to land on. I'll liquify myself, then you can pick the loose cuff out of the puddle."

"You'll...what?"

"Don't worry, I do it all the time. Great way to hide from the maids when they're being snippy. Pippa can be *such* a bitch when she's tired of getting me mojitos."

"I...uh...really need to get you back to Evitankari. Your ambassador's waiting."

I put my hands firmly on my hips and fired up my best stink eye. Remember who serves as Talvayne's ambassador to Evitankari? "You are *not* taking me back to your second-rate city to turn me over to Twat Face Jr. No way. You know what happens if I return to Talvayne? I have to marry a fucking troll! Have you even met any trolls?"

Roger scratched his chin. "So those are real too?"

His response was so stupid it left me momentarily stunned. Who the hell was this guy, and how many times had he been dropped as an infant? "I'm not going back!" I shrieked, stomping my feet angrily. "Especially not because I got 'rescued' by some dopey human who wouldn't know a nymph from a wisp."

He blinked at me like a big, dumb cow. "What's a wisp?"

"You're kidding, right? A wisp—"

And that's when the sneaky bastard hit me in the face with a handful of the same damn dust he knocked Talora out with. I couldn't help inhaling a mouthful of the bitter crap. Did I get played? Oh yeah. Rest assured that when I become queen, Evitankari is *off* the guest list of all our summer parties.

I awoke sometime later to the sensation of someone brushing my hair away from my forehead. It reminded me of walking into the sort of low-hanging branch that gives easily and then snaps suddenly back into place once you're past. Guess why.

"Motherfucker," I growled. That strange human had made good on his promise. I'm sure it was all "mission accomplished!" and "Brownie, you're doing a heckuva job!" back in Evitankari. For yours truly, it was more along the lines of "I did not have sexual relations with that woman." I'd tried to beat the system and shirk my responsibilities and gotten caught red-handed.

"Welcome back," Twat Face Jr. hissed way too close to my ear. Gone from his voice was the overeager faux politeness that had always made me desperate for a shower. Dude was all blunt, angry business. That made me nervous.

"S-Sorrin?" I asked. Playing innocent seemed like the way to go. "Where am I? Are those terrible demons gone?"

"You're in Talvayne. And you can cut the shit."

I sat up quickly and opened my eyes. The thought of lying prone beside that scumbag suddenly felt like a worse idea than any of the Spice Girls' solo albums. My vision still hadn't completely rebooted, so the room around me was just an impossibly bright, green and white blob. To my left, Sorrin looked like a giant piece of shit smeared across the scene. Yeah, not that different from usual.

"I was just rescued from a group of vile, demented kidnap-pers," I replied. "The least you could do is show some empathy!"

Someone behind me snorted. Gaptorix. I'd know that expres-sion of disappointment via vibrating snot anywhere. So it was Twat Face Jr. and the violent, ultra-conservative captain of the guard. Talk about an unholy alliance.

"We know you ran," Sorrin snarled. "It's obvious who helped you. Lucky for us, your annoying friend isn't nearly as smart as she thinks she is."

I highly doubted that. Seemed to me she'd merely put her trust in the wrong lackey. No way things would've gone down this way if Talora had listened to Rayn's damn directions. I'm going to insist on consulting on all of my bestie's future minion hirings. Her interview process could obviously use some serious rethinking.

But I had more immediate concerns. "I demand you take me to my father this instant!" Not a great option, but probably my best. I can't remember the last time I'd actually wanted Lard Ass's help.

Sorrin chuckled. "That's the plan, princess. The king and I are overdue for a little chat."

I didn't like the sound of that. "You will take me to my father, you will graciously accept his thanks for the return of his daughter, and you will get out of my sight. If you fail to follow these simple instructions, I'm telling Fro to get the belt sander."

"See, boys?" Sorrin shouted. "This is what I like best about Myrindi: even being held hostage by a dozen heavily armed trolls can't dull her fiery sprit!" His voice turned sinister, the effect magnified by the way my fucked up vision twisted his face. "I'm really going to enjoy breaking that."

A shiver ran down my spine. "You've been practicing in the mirror, haven't you?" I snapped. "I can tell. Your evil shithead game is totally on point today."

"Take her," Sorrin commanded. He held up a red and black blob and tapped its side with his bulbous hand. Plastic. "And don't even think about liquifying yourself to try to get away. We brought the wet vac."

"My, my," I said dramatically, "you *have* thought of everything, haven't you?" He hadn't, of course. He's an idiot. I was sure escape would merely be an exercise in determining what he'd missed. A pair of wide, strong hands scooped me up like I was an infant. The side of my head rested uncomfortably against a bare troll chest. "Don't get grabby, Gaptorix," I growled.

"You're not my type," he replied.

The room around me swirled into motion. One of the trolls opened a smear that must've been a door and Sorrin led the way out into the hallway beyond. I recognized that cavernous corridor even without perfect vision: it was the Lambent Path, the main entrance to the throne room. Crystal statues of Talvayne's previous kings stand along either side, organized in order of their reigns, as a means of reminding us where we've been as we approach the throne room. Each glitters a slightly different array of colors meant to communicate the kings' personalities, though no one can really agree on what the individual colors mean. The hall itself physically expands as necessary even though the castle itself never grows around it. Given that Talvayan kings average about twenty years on the throne and we've been at this shit for awhile, it's kind of a long fucking walk.

Personally, I'm not a fan of the old LP. All those statues of the kings in various constipated poses always make me think of the queens. Maybe I'm biased, but I think that one room sums up Talvayne's issues pretty well. I avoid the Lambent Path whenever I can because it puts a knot the size of a grapefruit in my stomach. That time, carried across the marble by the hulking Gaptorix, the effect was even worse. I couldn't help wondering what stupid pose Sorrin would insist on for his own statue. Would he go for thoughtful and rapey, imposing and rapey, merciful and rapey, or just rapey and rapey? If Twat Face Jr. got his way, he'd be immortalized forever as one of Talvayne's kings. He'd rule until marrying off our daughter, then he'd get a fucking statue and a cushy lifetime fucking position in the Conclave of Kings. He'd be someone important not just for the remainder of his miserable life but for-fucking-ever. History would forget *how* he became king and focus instead on some stupid bridge he built, some piddly change he made to the tax code, or some heartfelt speech he gave that just happened to be conveniently written by an aid good at such drivel. Meanwhile, I'd perpetuate the whole whack-ass cycle without so much as a thank you card or a fruit basket in return. I'd be just like all the queens that came before me: gone and forgotten, a tool that served its purpose and then broke down. Fuck you, Diary.

The troll guards standing watch outside the throne room kicked in the double doors at our approach and then fell into step beside Sorrin's little coup. Lard Ass glared up at us from the Throne of Light, interrupted in mid-sentence while addressing a slimy water nymph petitioner wearing a track suit that just screamed "I'm not allowed within 100 feet of a school zone." Yeah, my vision had mostly cleared. Really glad that dude was one of the first things I got to see properly again. Thanks again for the knockout dust, Pintiri Roger Brooks.

"What is the meaning of this?" Father rumbled like the powerful, pissed off, take-no-prisoners monarch I desperately needed him to be but knew deep down he could only kind of imitate. No one in Sorrin's posse acknowledged the king. I could feel Gaptorix stifle a laugh.

Time to at least try to turn on the innocence. "Daddy!" I squeaked. "These evil men kidnapped me and won't let me go!"

My voice summoned Fro from a chamber to the left of the throne. I've never been so happy to see his big, ugly face. Sorry, Fro. He scanned my captors anxiously, searching for a solution and obviously finding none. Still, his mere presence in the throne room made rescue feel so much closer. If Lard Ass couldn't find a way to turn the tables, surely my loyal Froman would figure something out.

"Yo, dudes!" the greasy petitioner protested with all the force of a regional manager who smokes too much dope on the weekend. "This is *my* time with the king. Wait your turn."

Yup, they killed him. One of the trolls walked up to the poor fool, grabbed his head, and snapped his neck. I screamed for effect as he crumpled to the marble floor. My shriek was shrill enough to make Gaptorix flinch. I'm still proud of that.

"What in the Rot do you think you're doing?" Lard Ass bellowed. It would've been more convincing if his voice hadn't cracked and if he hadn't already asked a similar question. Sometimes he got a little stuck when he couldn't immediately determine how to deal with something. Oh well.

"I know you're not particularly bright, but you can't be that stupid," Sorrin snapped. I kind of agreed with him.

Father snorted. "Myrindi is betrothed to another. You had your chance and you broke our deal at the first sign of difficulty. I'll thank you to leave her with me and get out of my sight." Better, but still not perfect.

"I don't think the other side of the latest bargain for your daughter's hand is going to come through anytime soon," Sorrin snarled.

The group stopped, now just a few feet from the dais supporting the Throne of Light. One of the trolls in the back of the pack stepped forward and raised a burlap sack before the king. With a vicious sneer, the troll flipped the sack upside-down and shook its contents out onto the floor. Dremellon's head fell out first, followed by his mother's and then his father's. Each landed on the stone with a sickening splat, rolled around a little, and then came to rest. Dremellon looked even goofier without his stunted body. Father blanched. Fro tensed. I considered peeing on Gaptorix and then decided to just scream again instead.

"You expect me to negotiate with kidnappers and murderers?" Lard Ass croaked.

"Not really," Sorrin said. One of the trolls handed him a golden staff topped with a bulbous cluster of malformed gemstones—rubies, emeralds, sapphires, diamonds, the works. The thing didn't shine or glitter, but rather seemed somehow darker and duller than its surroundings. I didn't like the look of that staff. It totally didn't go with Sorrin's outfit.

"Then what do you want?" Father asked.

Sorrin paused, pretending to consider this. "I want you off my throne."

Before Lard Ass could protest, Sorrin reached out with the staff and touched its gnarled head to the king's hand. The gemstones flared with dull light like some sort of depressed rainbow. Father's eyes went wide with pain and terror, and his lips opened to unleash a scream that never came. His flesh turned gray and dry, cracking and splintering into tiny flakes that fell from his body like gentle snow. The king's hefty frame collapsed in on itself as his weakened tissue could no longer support itself. Next time I blinked, King Luminad XIII had been reduced to a pile of ash lying atop the Throne of Light beneath a set of size XXXL royal robes. Kind of impressive when you think about it.

My heart seized. Lard Ass had always been a douchebag, but he was my father, damn it. I guess that's why the douchebaggery always hurt so much. Fuck you, Diary.

Sorrin turned to me and spun his staff triumphantly. He almost dropped it halfway through. "Neat, huh?" he chirped happily. "The Staff of Forinex. Part of the Rapgallaviks' payment for the honor of marrying their runt to a princess. Before the Great Bhangoo got a hold of it, the trolls of old deployed it as the ultimate punishment for their worst criminals, depriving them of the honorable death by combat their race traditionally seeks. Nothing particularly poetic about its use in this case, but it did the job, right?"

I couldn't bring myself to speak. My ability to generate a cool, snappy comeback had gone into hiding. One of the trolls stepped around Sorrin, wet vac in hand. He flipped the power switch and went to work cleaning the throne with a brush attachment. I'm not sure I'll ever forget the sound of my father's component particles rattling against the inside of that plastic tube.

Sorrin turned to Fro. My protector still hadn't moved. "Froman!" the wood nymph shouted. "I didn't see you there! Tell me: where do you stand on all this?"

"My only loyalty is to the life of the princess," he said flatly. "I've taken a sacred oath to protect the female side of the royal line. Nothing else matters." Way to make me feel even worse about running off, Fro.

Sorrin tapped his foot, considering his options. "She will be safest locked in her own chambers while I attend to the remainder of my business."

Fro nodded. "A fair assessment. May I escort the princess?"

"You may." Sorrin turned to his men. "Gaptorix, dispatch a squad to assist. Princess Myrindi is not to leave her rooms until the day of our wedding."

Times like that one really made me wish Rayn had a cell phone or a Facebook or at least a mailing address.

— CHAPTER NINE —

Pike stared longingly at the bottle of cheap beer in his hand as if it were the last bottle of beer in the entire world. Cool moisture dappled its long, slender neck like morning dew on freshly cut grass. He didn't recognize the red and yellow label, but he really didn't care. After all the bullshit he'd had to deal with since arriving in Talvayne—fighting trolls, having a ceiling dropped on his head, and babysitting the dump's intolerable wench of a princess—that bottle of beer was the most beautiful thing he'd ever seen.

"That's just booze, you know," Lep cracked from the other side of the table. "Rayn's not in there."

"Fuck you," Pike replied, not unhappily. He raised the bottle to his lips, ready to let the frosty beverage wash his cares away—at least for a few minutes.

That's when the entire room shook violently, up and down and side-to-side all at once. The earth itself seemed to groan. Pictures fell from the walls. Sculptures crashed from their pedestals. Glasses, plates, and mugs clattered against each other in the nearby cabinet, several shattering. Empty chairs rattled across the wood floor. From the bathroom on the level below, Myrindi shrieked. And half of Pike's beer spilled out onto his shirt.

The earthquake only lasted a few seconds. When it ended, those gathered in the dining room glanced at each other nervously. Fro ran off to check on the princess.

"Motherfucker," Pike growled as he slurped up the foam spewing out of his bottle.

"That a common occurrence in these parts?" Lep asked.

At the head of the table, Anstrum shook his head thoughtfully and surveyed the damage to his home. Old and withered and bent, Gol's father nonetheless radiated a certain power and virility missing in many men a fifth his age. Fierce intelligence and something a bit whimsical burned in glassy white eyes under his heavy brow. Clumps and nodules of darker dirt puckered his skin, as happens to sand nymphs of extreme age. Despite their differences in size and youth, Pike had no doubt the old man could find a way to take him down in a straight up fight.

"The land aches for a king," Anstrum said sagely. In his gritty, soft voice, that statement rang with absolute truth.

"Seriously?" Pike grumbled. "Great time to hide out in an underground house."

"Just as the magic of the princess keeps the Rot in check, the magic of the king maintains the rigid boundaries between Talvayne's different ecosystems," Gol explained as she gathered the pictures that had fallen off the wall. "Without a king, the land strains to reset itself."

"I knew all this couldn't be natural," Chastity mused. She sat beside Lep, his right hand clenched protectively in her left atop the table.

"Well that's fucking stupid," Pike muttered. He'd pulled his shirt up over his face in an attempt to suck the beer out of it.

Lep reached over and playfully poked his friend in the stomach. "Look at what you're doing right now and then reevaluate that statement."

"Many ideas that seem wise at the time become less so with age," Anstrum said. "But we must account for them still."

"So we marry the brat off to some poor schlub on our way out of town," Pike suggested. "Problem solved."

Anstrum chuckled, his smile revealing a set of teeth alternately yellow or missing. "It's not that simple. The land will only accept a king married to the queen in the throne room of the Palace of Light. The entire building is a focus designed to channel the necessary magic to bind the king to the land and allow him to bypass the magic that protects the princess's virginity."

"I'm not convinced this is our problem," Lep said. "We were paid to get Myrindi out of Talvayne, not to save the whole damn city."

Pike wasn't so sure of that, but he kept his mouth shut. Rayn had obviously positioned them in Talvayne for something important, and tricking them into a larger task by starting with a smaller one would be just her style.

"Removing Myrindi from the city limits under the current circumstances could spell the end of Talvayne," Anstrum said. "The land will tear itself apart without a king, and then the Rot will take whatever remains."

Which also seemed right up Rayn's alley, Pike thought.

"Hell of a decision," Lep grunted. Chastity squeezed his hand.

Pike nodded slightly in agreement and sucked some more beer out of his shirt. "Thanks a lot, Rayn," he whispered.

Dear Diary,

I interrupt this regularly scheduled flashback into my shitty-but-still-cute-and-inspiring life to bring you an important announcement. Trust me, you'll want to set your DVR for this one.

Oh. My. Fucking. God. Gol's. Brother. Is. A. Dreamboat!

I was climbing out of the shower when the earthquake hit. That bastard knocked my feet right out from under me. The tile floor was cold and hard and generally not ready to catch me in anything resembling a gentle manner. Naturally I yelped a rather un-princess-like yelp when my nonexistent ass collided with the floor. I swear the impact almost shoved my spine up into my brain. That quake could've succeeded where Dr. Neltsin had failed if it had just tried a little bit harder.

When the world stopped shaking, a quick knock on the door snapped me back to reality. "Princess? Are you all right in there?" His voice was soft and caring and warm, but also deep and strong and dripping with testosterone. Something I never knew was inside me melted. I worried my appendix had burst. "Princess?" the voice came again, like a ray of vibrant sunlight slicing through an ominous black storm cloud. He tried the knob, but I'd locked the door. "If you're okay, say so. Otherwise I'm knocking this door down."

Oh my. I felt my face flush, warm and purple. I worried that the stress of the last few days had somehow burst all the capillaries in my cheeks. As badly as I wanted to see this stud muffin bulldoze an unsuspecting door on his way to rescuing me from the big, bad earthquake, I was also lying naked on the floor of his cramped bathroom. The Royal Decency must be protected.

"I'm...uh...okay," I stammered, confused by my inability to efficiently complete a sentence. "I'll...be right there."

I stood on wobbly, unsure legs and plucked a fluffy purple towel from the nearby rack. I'd given Gol's mother my clothes and she'd promised to bring me a fresh outfit. Part of me was glad she hadn't. Wrapping myself in that towel would give me just the right combination of innocence, vulnerability, and sex appeal to make one hell of an introduction. Yes, this is the point in the story when I become a hormonal, smitten teenage girl. Deal with it, Diary. It's the least you can do after all the delicious dirt I've handed you.

My naughty bits thus covered, I unlocked the door, eased it open a few inches, and peered out. I came face-to-chest with a gorgeous hunk of man looking down at me with legitimate concern in his smoldering white eyes. Gol's brother looks like an award-winning sand sculpture inspired by the men in a fashion magazine. Dude's ripped. His tight blue jeans screamed in agony as his muscular thighs tried to burst free from their denim prison. A black T-shirt showed off just enough of his bulging shoulders and what could only be a set of washboard abs. His dark hair was cut short and strategically mussed in the front. The thick brow he'd inherited from his father and his mother's soft mouth and chin combined to give him a sort of triangular face that...well...yeah. I'm going to stop before you lose all respect for me.

His gaze drifted oh so slowly to my exposed shoulder, lingered for a moment, and then snapped back up to my face. My left leg shook so I hid it behind the door. I worried that I'd blown out my ACL when I fell.

"I don't think we were introduced earlier," he said. "My name's Sharn."

Sharn. Hard and rough, but kind of classy. It would look good on a business card. It would look better next to my name on a wedding invitation. "I'm Myrindi, Crown Princess of Talvayne."

He smiled. "I've heard. I was there the day you visited the Rot. You were...amazing."

Damn right I was. For some reason I couldn't bring myself to say so. "Thanks," I croaked. "It smelled pretty bad out there."

That got me a deep, friendly chuckle. "I'm pretty sure that was just the kings shitting themselves."

We both laughed. It felt good. It's not often I get to laugh *with* someone rather than just *at* someone. We'd known each other for approximately 80 seconds and yet I somehow felt more comfortable with Sharn than I felt with anyone, even Rayn.

His expression suddenly shifted. I couldn't parse it until he'd finished speaking. "Sounds like you've been through a lot today. How are you holding up?" he asked. That was concern, real and raw. I could tell he actually cared. I've been surrounded by phonies for so long that meeting someone genuine is like accidentally looking right at the sun. It's jarring. I probably would've stumbled if I hadn't been clutching the edge of the door.

"I've been better," I admitted. Being Princess Myrindi had certainly become difficult lately. It bothered me that this random dude was the first person to show legitimate concern for my emotional well-being.

"If you need to talk about it, I'm around," he said. "Or we can just watch TV and forget about it all. Whatever works best."

My stomach did a backflip and twisted itself into a French braid. I worried that I'd never be able to eat solid food ever again. Our eyes met and something passed between us, something neither science nor magic can completely account for, something I'd always suspected was probably just a great big load of bullshit. All of a sudden all I wanted to do was run my hands over his perfectly sculpted body while his powerful arms held me tight.

"Princess!" Fro shouted, appearing to my right at the far end of the hallway. He rushed toward us, clearly out of breath. Trolls aren't made for spiral staircases.

The moment ruined, Sharn flashed me a quick wink. "See you at dinner," he said as he turned and walked back down the hallway to his own room. He's got a nicer butt than me. That's just not fair.

Fro took Sharn's place at the bathroom door. "Princess!" he hissed again. "You weren't harmed during the quake, were you?" He glanced suspiciously toward Gol's departing brother and lowered his voice. "Was that man trying something untoward?"

I slammed the door in Fro's face and slumped to the floor. With Sharn gone, I could suddenly be myself again. "I'm fine, Froman!" I snapped. "But I'd be a hell of a lot better with some clothes and a latte!"

— CHAPTER TEN —

The attack came mere moments after Gol's mother set the roast down on the dining room table. No one heard the front door open, but none of them missed the rhythmic clang of a grenade bouncing down the steps. It exploded before any of them could react, unleashing a puffy cloud of yellowish smoke that expanded in all directions.

Anstrum, seated at the head of the table, was the first to his feet. "Everybody out the back," he said calmly. "Sharn, show them the way."

No one argued. Sharn led them out of the dining room through the kitchen, then the living room, and into a small foyer trimmed with blue and white wallpaper. He lingered by the door, a round, windowless hatch set in the angled outer wall, and waited for Pike and Lep to ready their weapons. Froman hung close to the princess. Anstrum clutched both his wife's hand and his daughter's. Chastity brought up the rear, her eyes on the growing cloud behind them. The group barely fit in that small room.

"You know they want us leaving this way, right?" Lep asked.

"No shit," Pike grumbled.

"Just wanted to make sure you're paying attention."

"Pay attention to this. Chas, blow the door."

Chastity stepped up through the crowd to stand beside Pike. She took a second to compose herself, then she thrust her hands forward and cast a spell that sent the door and a good section of the wall flying off into the sky.

"The crown will pay for the damage," Myrindi said to Anstrum. "And for some wallpaper that isn't older than I am."

Pike leapt out into the surrounding patch of desert as soon as the way was clear, his broadsword swinging in a huge arc that took one troll in the neck and sent another ducking for cover. Lep followed, casually dropping the troll Pike missed with a throwing knife between the eyes and then side-stepping the mad rush of another. Chastity caught that one in her telekinetic grip before it could fall through the hole and into the mud room. She spun it around once, humming to herself, and then sent him rocketing into his remaining companion. The two big elves pounced on them quickly. Pike beheaded his target with one swing of his mighty broadsword. Lep did the deed with a dagger through the eye.

"I figured there'd be more," Pike growled as he surveyed the area.

The others clambered out into the desert to escape the smoke. Anstrum's land was a peaceful patch of gently billowing sand and hot, stifling air. It abutted a frigid arctic tundra to the east, a dense rain forest to the north, and a roiling black storm cloud to the west. To the south, beyond the dune that essentially served as the house's roof, was the brick and mortar street. The borders of the four properties, once so solid and well-defined, had begun bleeding into each other. Pockets of ice, tangled vines, and specks of cloud littered the outskirts of Anstrum's plot. His sand and sunshine likewise speckled his neighbors' land like miniature deserts.

Froman left the princess's side and knelt beside the nearest of the four corpses. He examined a length of yellow twine wrapped around its left wrist. "Remlaar," he gasped, standing abruptly. "The Tip of the Spear. Men and women deemed fit only to die."

"So?" Pike asked.

"So this was a feint."

Lep took a few steps away from the rest of the group and anxiously scanned the surrounding lots. "Where the fuck are they?"

"Helloooooooooooo!" a high-pitched voice squealed.

Gol shrieked and stumbled. Myrindi stepped behind Fro. The elves turned to face the newcomer, weapons at the ready.

"Hi there," Chastity said hesitantly.

A purple and white wisp zipped out of the the giant storm cloud next door. A creature of air and light, it looked like some sort of semi-translucent fireball roiling gently around a brightly lit center. "Hiiiiiiii!" it continued. "What's all the ruckus about, Anstrum?"

"Don't worry about it, Mrs. Lacklen," the old sand nymph replied. "Just a few unwelcome visitors."

She zipped closer. "Why, those are the king's guards!" she squealed. "And that's the princess! Are you kidnapping the princess? You brutes!"

"Don't worry about it, Mrs. Lacklen," Anstrum repeated. "It's nothing. Go home."

The wisp flared brightly. "Oh! Nothing, is it? Nothing! Like all the sand of yours that's suddenly popping up on my lawn? Like that campfire that got out of control last summer? Like that time your son knocked over my garbage can with his skateboard?"

"That was ten years ago," Sharn muttered.

Mrs. Lacklen wasn't done. "Like when I hired your daughter to feed my cat for a week while I vacationed and Mr. Fluffernutter gained three pounds? Like those trolls that paid me to look the other way when they buried themselves on your land? Like—"

"Hold up!" Pike shouted. "What trolls?"

A burly green hand shot up out of the sand and grabbed Lep's ankle. A quick twist and a sickening snap and it was broken. The big man fell to the ground, screaming and slashing wildly with his dagger.

All around them, trolls in full armor pulled themselves up out of the sand. Pike and Froman closed ranks around Myrindi as Chastity rushed to her husband's side. Her fingertips flared with deadly energy as she grabbed the wrist of Lep's attacker. The buried troll spasmed with pain and released Lep's foot.

"It's about time!" Mrs. Lacklen tootled. "Arrest these princess-stealing hooligans!"

"Thanks a lot, neighbor," Sharn grumbled.

"You got it backwards, bitch!" Myrindi added.

Mrs. Lacklen did a backflip in the air. "Well, I never! Such *language*! And from royalty!"

Gaptorix burst from the sand beside Chas and Lep in all his loinclothed glory. He swatted the small woman aside with one mighty backhand. She crashed into the sand and didn't get back up. "Turn yourselves in and King Sorrin will show mercy!" he bellowed.

"King Sorrin?" Myrindi asked. "Phhhhhhhhhhhhhhhhh-hhhhhhhhhhht!" She added an eye roll and a wanking motion for good measure.

Fro took a few steps toward the captain of the guard. Myrindi's protector was about half Gaptorix's size. "Why ally yourself with that vile murderer?" Fro asked. "He is beneath our kind. He has no honor."

"Plus he's a dildo," Myrindi added.

Gaptorix ignored her. "Honor is a funny word coming from your tongue, Froman. Every year the Conclave outlaws more and more of our people's sacred traditions. As the only troll among them, you should be using your position to protect our ways. Instead, you forsake your duty to babysit a succession of spoiled brats, each worse than the last. What do you know of *honor*?"

"Hold on," Myrindi gasped. "Fro? You're a king? You're my *grandfather*?"

"Put the word 'great' in front of that twenty or so times, Princess," the old troll replied. "Gaptorix...some traditions aren't worth saving. My time protecting the princesses has taught me that much."

Gaptorix's bulbous lips curled into a sneer. "I'm going to enjoy tearing your head off, you rabbit hugging, flower sniffing, cranberry licking—"

"Fuck, you people need to work on your insults," Myrindi snapped. She stepped between the two trolls and pointed Rayn's pinwheel squarely at the captain of the guard. "My bestie gave me this in the restroom by the archives. Yeah, remember the woman who buried you in charcuterie? Her! Screw off and tell Sorrin to take a flying leap or I swear I'll use this thing. Oh, and you really ought to consider wearing pants. Maybe a nice pair of black slacks. Something you can stick a few socks in to hide what all those steroids did to you."

A brisk cheer rose up from nearby. Perhaps twenty people had gathered along the street side of Anstrum's property to watch the proceedings. Myrindi acknowledged them with a regal wave.

Gaptorix was not impressed. "The Witch gave you a pinwheel? Congratulations. She gave King Sorrin an alliance with my trolls."

"You're full of shit."

Gaptorix smiled, revealing his crooked, blocky teeth. "She's been playing you all along, little fool. All you are and all you have ever been—to anyone—is a walking, talking ticket to the throne."

Thunder rumbled in the distance. Myrindi turned slightly to glower at Pike. The big elf, eyes wide, just shook his head and shrugged. The crowd by the street, which had begun inching closer to the action as more and more passersby joined its ranks, unleashed a torrent of boos and catcalls.

"That's not very nice," Mrs. Lacklen grumbled.

Myrindi turned back to Gaptorix and smiled. "Let's see which side Rayn's *really* on."

She glared slow, fiery death at the hulking troll as she took a deep breath, raised the pinwheel to her lips, and blew as hard as she could. The toy's flimsy leaves whirled to life, clicking and clacking as only a cheap piece of crap grandma should've left in the bargain bin at the dollar store can click and clack. Nothing of note happened, so Myrindi strained herself to blow even harder. Gaptorix crossed his arms and chuckled evilly. In the distance, thunder boomed even louder.

The princess, her face purple, finally ran out of breath about twenty seconds later. The pinwheel didn't give up with her, however. It somehow spun faster in response. Silver sparks popped and fizzled in its center. One by one each leaf burst away from the pinwheel's axle to flitter around Myrindi. Each took on a slightly different color as it orbited the princess. Soon she was encased in a cylinder of kaleidoscopic light. The crowd, now mere feet away and bigger than ever, roared its approval. Gaptorix and his befuddled trolls didn't dare move.

And then the light show died. The leaves flared brightly one last time and then tumbled gently to the ground, reduced to useless ash. Myrindi dropped the pinwheel's stick and lowered her head, letting her long black hair hide her tears from the crowd as she fought back sobs. Dense gray clouds rolled in overhead, bringing with them a sprinkle of heavy raindrops.

"I told you so," Gaptorix said happily. The desert between his bare feet began to swirl like a tiny hurricane. "Last chance, Princess. Surrender now or all of your friends will die slowly—"

The sand beneath him erupted upward, forming a manly fist and a well-defined arm as it rocketed toward Gaptorix's nether regions. Sharn's dashing face winked at Myrindi from the dirt just as his knuckles collided with the guard captain's equipment. The troll gasped and bent forward, his face an impossible shade of red. The crowd groaned in mock sympathy. Gaptorix's legs quivered, but he somehow kept himself on his feet. Job done, Sharn collapsed back into the desert and disappeared.

Lightning struck somewhere near by. "Fro," Myrindi growled, "do you remember when I was six and we played knights versus dragons in the Glittering Gardens?"

"Vividly," the old troll said, confused.

"Remember how we 'killed' the tree I said was the evil dragon?"

Fro smiled. He grabbed the princess's shoulder with his left hand, gripped her belt with his right, and lifted her off her feet. Spinning like a shot putter, Fro whipped Myrindi around and released her at the completion of his turn, hurling the tiny princess toward their vulnerable enemy. She liquified just before she collided with Gaptorix's broad face, pulling her watery form into the troll's gaping mouth and down his esophagus. She solidified part of a finger to push open the valve protecting the beast's single lung—his species's most infamous vulnerability—and poured herself inside. Stunned and unable to breathe but still a bad motherfucker, Gaptorix punched himself over and over again in the stomach in an attempt to force Myrindi out. The liquified princess stuck herself to the fleshy folds of his lung with every ounce of willpower she could muster. Pike and Froman stepped between Gaptorix and his men, fighting wildly to give Myrindi the time she needed to finish the guard captain off. Sharn burst from the sand here and there to trip up the onrushing trolls.

Gaptorix finally drowned to death two and a half minutes later. His body went slack and he collapsed sideways like a falling redwood, tossing up a shower of sand when he landed. Myrindi streamed back out through his nostrils and returned to her normal form. The crowd roared. Myrindi, who'd forgotten that she'd shed her clothing during her initial trans-formation, raised her arms in triumph and smiled viciously. Nude, covered head-to-toe in slimy mucus, her hair sticking out at odd angles and her eyes burning wildly, the fashionable Crown Princess of Talvayne looked like she had been replaced by a demon unleashed from the depths of some watery hell. Her subjects loved it. She felt like the world's biggest rock star. The rain stopped and the ominous clouds above dissipated into thin white tendrils.

"Oh, princess!" a gravelly troll voice shouted from behind her. "I hate to interrupt, but there's something you really ought to see."

Myrindi turned. Though they'd incapacitated half a dozen trolls, Fro and Pike had lost the fight. The elf lay prone and gasping, bleeding from a jagged wound in his side. Fro was on his knees, his face criss-crossed with shallow cuts and his left arm hanging limp. One of Gaptorix's men held a dagger to his throat.

The princess didn't even flinch. She stomped right up to the troll who'd taken command and chewed him out, punctuating every word by jamming her finger against his steel breastplate. She stood on her tip-toes so she could better look him in the eye. "Listen up, you green piece of shit," she snarled. "I'm the motherfucking Crown Princess of Rot-damned Talvayne. Do you know what that means? It means I'm fucking in charge. You will release my protectors and vacate the premises right the fuck now or I will see to it that every last one of you illiterate, filthy, poorly dressed traitors joins your captain in whatever hell you fucking barbarians invented to maintain your simpering culture of mindless thuggery. You've got three fucking seconds."

Several of the trolls glanced at each other uncertainly. Their leader actually took a short step away from the enraged princess mid-tirade, then gathered himself and drew a heavy-duty zip tie from his pocket. "Your hands, Princess. Your hands or their heads."

The crowd had begun to grumble. Myrindi couldn't help flashing back to that day her subjects had cheered her as she strolled through the Rot while the kings crapped themselves. She'd been here before. Sensing the tide of energy waiting to be unleashed, she knew what she had to do—and she knew she'd already won.

She tried to spit in the guard's eye but hit his chin instead because she wasn't tall enough. "You are an honorless runt who can't lift his own sword. Your mother eats strawberries. Your father only has one tiny testicle and loves to read self-help books. Every woman you bed can't wait to tell her friends how soft and smooth your thighs are. Your sister—"

That's when the troll made his fatal mistake. Enraged, he rammed his massive left fist into Myrindi's gut. His knuckles were hard as stone. She doubled over and then dropped, fighting for the breath her assailant had driven from her body.

"You shall *not* harm our princess!" a ragged voice shouted from the crowd, somehow sounding angry and saddened and confused all at once. A hail of threats and war cries seconded the original outburst. Myrindi, her eyes shut tight against the pain in her gut as she struggled to breathe, didn't see the mass of people that surged over and around her to overwhelm the remaining trolls, but she sure felt it. The desert in which she lay echoed with outraged, righteous footfalls. Metal clashed against metal. Shouts of triumph and shrieks of pain sliced through the background static of wild battle.

Myrindi tried to fight back tears and failed miserably. She hoped she hadn't doomed Fro and that Pike would survive his wound, but not without a gruesome scar that would frighten little children and itch like a motherfucker. She willed Sharn to stay safely hidden in the sand. She wanted to knight Lep and Chastity. She really, really wanted to punch Rayn in the face. She wished her mother was there.

Two pairs of gentle hands lifted Myrindi up and carried her away from the action. She groaned at the pain that racked her torso. "You're safe now, Princess," a warm, feminine voice whispered in her ear. "Your people have you."

Squeezing her eyes shut even tighter, Myrindi nodded weakly. Her tongue felt useless. She wasn't made for moments like this one.

But years later, those who fought for the princess would still marvel at the brightness and warmth of the sun, the way the gentle breeze soothed their injuries, the way the air itself and the land beneath their feet seemed to caress them in thanks.

Dear Diary,

I killed a troll today. Not just any troll, mind you, but the biggest, baddest bastard in all the land: Gaptorix. I *know*, right? I drowned him! With myself! It was soooooooooo icky. I've showered three times in the hours since and I swear I still smell him. I've acquired a permanent musk of sweat and salami. Thanks a lot, Gaptorix.

The big goof and his trolls ambushed us at Anstrum's. I'm still not sure how they knew we were there. My would-be protectors are a mess. Fro's got a broken arm and a few scars-in-training on his face. Lep's on crutches. Pike took a battle axe to the side and might lose a kidney. Chastity should have a concussion and a broken jaw but she somehow seems more damaged mentally and emotionally than physically. Me? Just a giant bruise on my stomach. I definitely won that exchange; the head of the troll who hit me is atop a spear outside the guard barracks my loyal subjects took as our new anti-Sorrin HQ. It hurts whenever I move too quickly or breathe too deeply, but that's nothing compared to the dueling pains in my heart. That's right, Diary, I'm about to get all emotional and introspective. Grab some tissues and warm up the waaaahmbulance in case I overdo it.

First off, it turns out Rayn was never really my bestie. She played the role to a T, but it was all an act. She brokered the unholy alliance between Twat Face Jr. and Gaptorix's trolls that led to my father's death and all the bullshit that's gone down since. That pinwheel she gave me fired off a useless light show—pretty, but useless. I know Rayn, so I know that was a statement. About me. Fun to look at but ultimately vapid and powerless. That bitch.

Part of me still can't accept that I've been betrayed. After all, why would Rayn have sent Lep's crew to aid me if all she wanted to do was screw me over? Why let me escape my quarters after Sorrin murdered my father? Why not just hand me over to Gaptorix when she found me in the restroom near the archives? And what the hell was up with that trip to Beijing? An annoying little voice in the back of my mind insists that none of it made any sense, but I manage to mentally shout it down every time it gets mouthy. Rayn's not one to merely accomplish something. Everything she does, she does with style. She has more layers than my father's favorite sheet cake. I know she's set up something else waiting to punch me in the vagina, something she thinks I'll never see coming. Maybe Chas is a walking bomb. Maybe Lep is really a portal to another dimension where they never invented cashmere. Maybe Pike knows how to read. I've been racking my brain to identify Rayn's next angle and defuse it, but I'm drawing one hell of a frustrating blank.

All that's just my first problem. The second...I can't believe is even an issue. It's something I've both always wanted and always assumed was just sort of happening anyway, but being slapped in the face with it is different than dreaming it or lying to your vapid friends about it. So, problem number two: Talvayne fucking loves me.

When Gaptorix's trolls had me cornered outside Anstrum's, my subjects came running to my aid. Perhaps that's too sterile a description; they washed over my enemies like a Rot tsunami, leaving nothing but pieces and parts behind. And then they swept into the nearest barracks, killed the traitors they found inside, and presented me with a new base from which I can conduct the civil war to claim the palace and my place on the throne.

I'm having a difficult time wrapping my head around that loyalty. I don't think I've ever spoken to any of these people before, although several claim to have met me at minor gatherings or witnessed my stroll through the Rot. I know I'm the princess and thus Talvayne is supposed to worship me, but I always figured it was a lip service sort of thing for most people, like loving your in-laws or donating to charity; everybody says they do it and they go through the motions when they have to, but it's primarily driven by social pressure. Apparently that's not actually the case.

Two old women—a sylvan named Loris who smells like eggs and a chain-smoking gnoll with one eye named Morenith—took charge of me after the fight at Anstrum's. The pair hovered around me like a pair of mother hens, steering me away from the violence and keeping nosy Talvayans at bay while I composed myself. Morenith even shooed Fro away at one point and insisted that he get help for his own injuries before worrying about mine. They put some sort of salve on my bruised midsection, dressed me in a soft brown bathrobe (don't ask), and tried to help me get the mucus out of my hair (double don't ask) as the city rioted around me.

Loris and Morenith led me to the barracks after my people had secured it, each holding one of my hands. I still didn't quite have my shit together. My head was spinning and I fought the urge to throw up with every step. Those in the streets stepped aside as we approached, lining both curbs like a crowd watching a parade. Many were injured. Some cried. Others brandished weapons or armor or other more ghastly trophies taken from Gaptorix's trolls. Some of them waved, bowed, or nodded. They wouldn't stop *staring* at me. I mean, normally I like being looked at, but this was different. This was real. I wasn't just something pretty to admire anymore. I was a reason to act, a rallying cry, a cause.

Morenith leaned her big ugly head close to mine and whispered in my ear. "I know you're still a little shaken up, Princess, but some acknowledgment would be polite."

She was right. These people had put their lives on the line for me without expecting anything in return. I don't know what to do with that. I waved weakly. The crowd cheered. I couldn't look at any of them.

A larger group awaited me in front of the barracks: the men and women who'd stormed the building in my name. All were smeared brown with blood and dirt and sweat and who knows what else. They looked tired but triumphant, ready to show off the property and lives they'd taken for their princess. A few could barely stand. I wondered where they were hiding those who hadn't made it. The barracks itself was a nondescript gray cube with narrow, barred windows and a single iron door hanging sideways from its busted hinges. Taking this big lump of concrete had not been easy.

I hesitated just a little when I noticed the troll standing in my subjects' midst. He wore the silver breast plate of one of the Royal Guard. Morenith noticed my change in pace and leaned close to my ear again. "He is with us. He kicked the front door open from the inside when he heard what his fellows tried to do to you."

A short, burly lycan in a basketball jersey and gym shorts pushed his way out of the crowd and into the street. He carried a short sword in each hand. His black and gray fur was matted with fluids I'd rather not think about. There was more warmth and intelligence in his beady black eyes than I expected in such a savage-looking creature. Picture a professional athlete rippling with lean muscle but covered in fur and topped with the head of a wolf. He smiled, revealing rows of sharp teeth under his lupine snout. One of his big, pointed ears was missing. I haven't met many lycans. Most of them serve in Talvayne's intelligence services or pimp themselves out as walking, talking fur suppliers. Even laser surgery can't keep the bastards smooth for more than a week.

"Princess," he growled, "we've captured this barracks in your name." He bowed his head and dropped to one knee on the cobblestones.

Everyone nearby mirrored his gesture. Hundreds of men, women, and children paid me silent salute without being asked to do so. Even Morenith and Loris took a step back and kneeled.

So where's the problem, right? Here's the truth, in case your stupid ass hasn't figured it out yet: the Princess Myrindi I've been for the majority of my sixteen years is all just part of my schtick. It's an act, like Pike's attempts to be a bad-ass or Rayn's affection for yours truly. Remember how my mother used to talk to me in the womb? She gave me a plan. A mission. An idea that could take my destiny as a magic uterus and transform it into a weapon. Mother told me all about the world and my place in it before I ever got a chance to experience it for myself. It sounded miserable. My time in the palace has done nothing to disprove that initial assessment. I lived surrounded by sycophants, schemers, power hungry sociopaths, and Fro. No offense, Fro, but you're not exactly a ball of fire. There were bright spots, sure—that birthday party with Jordan Knight, the day Nella and her trailer park family were exiled, a few really great pedicures, late nights talking fashion with Rayn—but for the most part, being Crown Princess of Talvayne sucks. Gaptorix wasn't completely wrong when he called me a walking, talking ticket to power. We princesses are tools, goods to be appraised and traded by men seeking to improve their standing. "They're going to make your life hell," Mother told me night after night as I floated inside her. "They don't want us for us. They don't us to be *people*. They want pretty, vapid, uncaring representations of wealth, power, and privilege. Give them what they want. Give it to them in spades."

So I did. I was born a bomb, primed and ready to explode over and over and over again. And I don't really know how to turn it off. Not even when I'm surrounded by people just trying to do right by me, who bled and fought and lost loved ones simply to protect me. I reflexively wanted to ask the lycan what took so long, why the barracks they'd taken was so small and ugly, and why the hell he'd thought wearing a burnt orange jersey was even remotely a good idea. I bit my tongue so hard it drew blood. I know my mother trained me this way for my own good because she loved the shit out of me, but sometimes I wonder if I'm nothing more than a bitter, dying woman's desperate attempt to exact a measure of revenge upon the people and the system that had doomed her to a short, joyless life. Fuck you, Diary.

Nothing Mother had taught me fit this situation. I'd always known exactly what to say in the palace because my best option was always just to be a haughty, stuck-up snot. It even worked with Rayn because she loved that shit. Spoiled princess just wouldn't cut it here.

"R-rise," I stammered, blushing purple. The lycan and the crowd obeyed in almost perfect synchronization. It was kind of scary. What I said next was even more frightening. It left me shaking. "Th-thanks," I whispered.

I doubt the lycan could've heard me at that distance. Maybe he read my lips. Regardless, I'll always be thankful for how he stopped what could've become a really awkward silence before it even started. With a roguish smirk on his furry face, he thrust his two swords into the air. "All hail Princess Myrindi!" he shouted. "Walker in the Rot! Slayer of trolls!"

"All hail Princess Myrindi!" the crowd repeated. "Walker in the Rot! Slayer of trolls!"

Which brought me to another moment demanding my earnest participation. I've never been earnest in my life. I'm still not sure I like it. The lycan's cheer made me realize something important: my subjects had gotten behind a spoiled princess that day in the Rot and back at Anstrum's at least in part because they agreed with my tactics and my targets. Maybe they would again.

"That fucking twit defiling *my* throne with his wooden ass is in for a rude fucking surprise!" I shrieked. The crowd roared. I gave the raucous noise a moment to die down naturally before continuing. "He's just a splinter in my toe! I'm taking my fucking palace back, and then I'm shoving 'King' Sorrin into the nearest wood chipper so I can use him as mulch in the Glittering Gardens!"

The ensuing cheer was even louder than the previous. Spurred forward by equal measures of adrenaline and embarrassment, I stomped toward the barracks without the help of Morenith and Loris. The crowd's energy dulled the pain in my gut. I touched the lycan's hairy elbow and he fell into step at my side.

"Your name?"

"Kres Renvy, Your Highness."

"Renvy, it seems to me I need a new captain of the guard. Interested in the position?"

He stumbled. "If it pleases Your Highness, yes."

"It sure as shit pleases My Highness. There's a comprehensive health and retirement package, but the first paycheck won't come until we've taken back the treasury."

"I suspect Your Highness is good for it."

"Damn straight." I nodded toward the lone troll, who looked as uncomfortable as a twelve-year-old boy at his first middle school dance—except, you know, seven feet tall and greener. "How do you feel about this guy?"

"We couldn't have taken this building without him, Your Highness."

"That's your new second in command," I said. "Now please show me to the ranking officer's quarters. I need a nap and a Rot damned shower."

"Yes, Your Highness."

But seriously—what the fuck am I supposed to do with these people? Can I let them just keep fighting and dying to put me back in the palace? And do my own hangups about that kind of thing really matter if that's what they legitimately want to do with themselves? Is it what I want, or am I letting them just carry me in that direction? I might have to be *nice* again, too.

Ugh. Fuck you, Diary.

— CHAPTER ELEVEN —

Myrindi woke to a heated argument outside the commander's quarters she'd taken as her own.

"I don't care what she said your title is or what door you opened," Sharn snarled. "You will let me see the princess."

Still groggy, Myrindi sat up on the hard cot and wiped the sleep out of her eyes. "It's all right, Rittenbrick. I'll see my guest in a few moments."

"Yes, Your Highness," he replied. The troll who'd turned on his fellows to help Talvayne's citizens take the barracks had taken to his new role in Myrindi's guard enthusiastically.

The princess tossed the rough blankets aside and swung her feet out onto the cold stone floor. Loris had left a change of clothes on a rickety wooden chair beside the bed. The commander's quarters had turned out to be a bit shabbier than Myrindi had expected. The room was downright tiny—about eight feet on each side—but its little round window and relative privacy on the top floor made it a definite upgrade over the rows of wooden bunks in the barracks' main hall. The room's previous owner hadn't bothered with any sort of decoration. The small desk in the corner was covered with maps of

Talvayne and a few requisition orders, most of it stained with coffee or speckled with crumbs. Myrindi made a mental note to ask Morenith to remove that desk and everything on it and light it all on fire.

Nothing fit. Loras had left her a pink T-shirt a size too small and a pair of flannel pants two sizes too big. Myrindi pulled the drawstring taut and tied it off in a tight knot. Loras had also included a purple scrunchy straight out of 1992. The princess flicked it into the garbage can under the desk and ran her fingers through her hair a few times. She hoped Sharn had a thing for the fresh-out-of-bed look.

After taking a further moment to compose herself, Myrindi unleashed her best confident royalty voice. "I will see the visitor."

Rittenbrick immediately swung the door open. Sharn flowed into the room, tall and strong and clean and perfect. Not a strand of hair nor a grain of sandy skin was out of place. Looking that good in the middle of an urban war zone is either a crime against humanity or grounds for a Nobel Prize. Rittenbrick slammed the door shut behind him.

"Princess," Sharn said formally, keeping his distance and standing at rigid attention. "Your people have captured two more barracks and a nearby armory. Sorrin's recalled his men to the safety of the palace, but not before he ordered all other properties of the Royal Guard put to the torch. We've got them on the run, Your Highness."

From anyone else, that would've been great news. From Sharn, well...a strategic update just wasn't what Myrindi wanted to hear. "Very good," she replied. "And your family?"

"All safe and healthy. Pop's downstairs trying to give self-defense lessons to your fighters. Mom and Gol are tending the wounded."

"And yourself?"

"Alive and proud to serve, Your Highness. Thank you for asking." He hesitated. "There is, however, one thing."

"Out with it. I encourage my people to speak freely." Myrindi wondered if he could hear her heart pounding in her chest.

"Well..." Suddenly he relaxed, smirked, and closed most of the space between them. "What you did out there was fucking awesome."

All the formality and tension was sucked out of the room as if somehow vented by the building's clunky old HVAC system. "I know!" Myrindi shrieked, hopping up and down and shaking her hands excitedly. "I mean, drowning Gaptorix was super gross, but still! And thanks for punching him in the nads!"

"It was my pleasure. And just so you know, it was a hell of a shot. I didn't exactly have a lot to aim for."

"Ever consider wearing a loincloth like that?"

"No."

"Good. But seriously, high-five!"

The collision of their palms echoed in the tiny room and set off a storm of butterflies in Myrindi's stomach. Rittenbrick knocked on the door. "Is everything okay in there, Princess?"

Myrindi and Sharn both doubled over with laughter. "We're fine!" the princess replied. "Watch that hallway, you hear? No telling who might be coming up that stairwell next!"

"Yes, Your Highness."

"Dude's worse than Fro," Myrindi muttered.

"I don't know how you stand it," Sharn said. He sat down on the bed. "The constant attention, having your every move watched and dissected, never truly being alone—that wouldn't work for me."

"It comes with the territory." She paused for a moment, slightly afraid to ask her next question. "Don't tell me you've never thought of being royalty."

"I bet it's impossible for anyone who's lived under a monarchy *not* to daydream about it from time to time. I think I'd be good at the job, but I can't say I actually *want* it. In fact, I'd say anyone that does should be kept as far away from the throne as possible."

"Hence our current predicament. Nobody wants to be king more than Twat Face Jr. It's pretty gross. Like a little wooden crackhead chasing his next fix."

"What about you?" Sharn asked, his interest obviously piqued. "Ever thought about *not* being royalty?"

"Not really," Myrindi replied somberly. "Always seemed like a waste of time. Even if I disappeared into the world somewhere, that whole I'm-the-only-one-who-can-stave-off-the-Rot thing would hang over my head like mistletoe at an office Christmas party where the weird dude from accounting is making drunken eyes at everything with a decent set of legs."

Sharn chuckled. "Been to a lot of those, have you?"

"I've watched a lot of TV." Myrindi immediately winced inside at her answer.

But the sand nymph just rolled with it. "Yeah, I hear you don't get out of the palace much, especially after that day in the Rot. Did you know you were invited to pretty much every party in the city for years after?"

Myrindi blushed and shook her head. "I had no idea."

"Everyone assumed your mail was being screened. Just made us do it all the more. Preschool graduation? Invite Princess Myrindi. Dog's third birthday? Invite Myrindi." Sharn paused. "Hell, I invited you to my quinceañero."

"Don't you mean quinceañera? Did you wear a pretty dress?"

"Nope, quinceañero. My friends and I invented a male version. Lots of video games and bench pressing random things we found in the house. I did three sets at six reps with Gol."

"She must've loved that."

Sharn shrugged. "My sister's a good sport. We've always been tight."

"I had a sister once. Sort of. We're not blood. Then she sold me out to Sorrin and Gaptorix. Fuck that bitch."

He frowned. "Sold you out? How?"

"Pretty sure she's been tracking my movements. She's persistent and crazy powerful. We had a chat in the ladies' room before I ran into Gol in the archives. That's where I got that useless pinwheel."

"And you haven't seen or heard from her since?"

"Nope. But she's shifty. She could've been there the whole time, or she could've been following my every move via an enchantment in that crappy toy."

"Sounds feasible. I'll be honest with you, Myrindi—I've been thinking about this a lot. It really bothers me that your enemies managed to hunt you down in my family's home. You should've been safe there. You're sure there's no other way Gaptorix could've located you?"

"It was Rayn. It had to be. The pinwheel was broadcasting our location..." The princess trailed off when an odd thought struck her. She took a moment to chew on it, considering the implications. "Oh, motherfucker," she finally muttered. "Where's Fro?"

"Downstairs with the others. Ma threatened to lock him in the jail cells if he didn't stop fussing and take some time to rest."

"Take me to him."

Sharn stood and headed for the door, frowning. "You think *Fro* gave away your hiding place?"

"Just go," Myrindi replied, waving him on with her fingers. She wasn't ready to give voice to her suspicions just yet—especially in front of Sharn. Maybe she wouldn't have to.

Rittenbrick looked at the pair in surprise and alarm as they stormed out into the hallway. "Princess?" the troll asked. He had a foot and about a hundred pounds on Froman, but he somehow seemed softer and less dangerous. Myrindi suspected he was related to the Rapgallaviks.

"Stay," she commanded. She wanted as few witnesses as possible. "That room isn't going to protect itself."

"Yes, Your Highness."

Ten steps down the hallway and they reached the spiral stairwell leading down to the barracks proper. Designed to make storming the command quarters and weapons storage on the top floor difficult, the staircase was a claustrophobic space barely wide enough for the average troll. Anyone ascending as Myrindi and Sharn made their way down would've had to turn sideways and press himself close to the wall to let them pass. Single bare bulbs hanging at the top and bottom landings cast just enough light to let them barely see where they were going. Under different circumstances, the princess wouldn't have minded lingering in such a tight, dark space with Sharn, but the desire to find Fro and dispel her worries drove her to almost run down those stone stairs.

They were a little more than halfway down when the earthquake hit. The sudden tremor threw off Myrindi's pace and her right foot clipped the back of her left leg. She squealed as she lost her balance and fell forward. With no railing to grab, visions of a nasty tumble down the hard stairs danced through the princess's mind. She was about to liquify herself to cushion the blow when Sharn's strong hand snagged her slender forearm. Momentum and inertia conspired to spin her into the wall, but she managed to get a hand up in time to keep her face from colliding with the rock. Sharn lost his balance and fell backwards, pulling Myrindi down with him. He landed right on his ass. She wound up in his lap, her back cradled in his chiseled left arm. She lingered there for just a moment before leaping back to her feet and continuing on her way.

"We really have to do something about these damn quakes," Sharn said, just a hint of disappointment in his tone. "There were three more while you were asleep."

Myrindi knew exactly how she wanted to solve that problem, but she kept it to herself. "The land aches for a king," she muttered.

The bottom of the stairwell opened into the corner of the barracks proper, a cavernous room that encompassed the majority of the building's ground floor save for the guard station near the door and the lavatory along the opposite wall. Myrindi's followers had turned the area into a makeshift field hospital. Bottom bunks were used to treat the wounded and injured while the tops were reserved for storage or those merely hoping to catch a quick rest. Few of either were empty. Volunteer nurses, doctors, and attendants flitted about like worker bees tending a hive while healthy fighters convened in ragged clusters to exchange stories and information or to strategize. With Sorrin's men on the run, many of those in the barracks could've easily returned to their own homes. That they hadn't spoke of a deep dedication to the princess or perhaps to a desire to be right in the middle of whatever was going to happen next. The barracks was loud, it smelled, and Myrindi kind of wished she were anywhere else.

Sharn stepped forward to lead the way. Myrindi stood up straight and sort of grimaced in an effort at grim determination. It mostly worked. She looked more like a nervous young girl trying to play the part and not quite getting it right, but that vulnerability suited those who noticed. Once again she found herself in a situation where a large group of people she didn't know expected something significant of her. Despite her upbringing, she'd never given much thought to what it really meant to be royalty. She suspected the same was true of most of the kings in their isolated little bubble world of fancy parties and backroom power plays. True responsibility had always been a foreign concept to Myrindi, a word used ironically to describe her contributions to Talvayne's fashion and culture. Turns out the real deal was a bigger burden than she ever could've imagined.

Of course, the princess's subjects couldn't let her just go about her business. Every single person she passed paused to briefly acknowledge her presence. Most just flashed her a knowing look and a nod or a wink. Some insisted on lightly touching her arms or shoulders. A few offered words of encouragement or blessing, the most heartwarming and gut-wrenching coming from the wounded. Myrindi moved through it all in a haze, treading lightly as if the floor beneath her next step might suddenly open up and try to swallow her. That these people had put their lives on the line for her once at Anstrum's had been shocking enough; that they seemed ready and willing to do so over and over and over again was downright frightening.

Sharn brought Myrindi to the back corner of the room. They found Fro and Lep huddled together over a hastily drawn map of the palace. His face wrapped in thick bandages and his arm in a sling and a cast, Fro nonetheless hopped right to his feet at the princess's approach. Lep remained on the floor beside his crutches. A thick walking boot covered his foot and ankle.

"It is good to see you well, Princess," Fro hissed. Myrindi had never heard him sound so tired. It made her even more hesitant to ask the question on her mind.

"This castle of yours is a tough bastard," Lep said. "No easy way in or out. Defensive enchantments all over the walls."

"It's never been taken by an outside force," Myrindi croaked. "Been a few thousand years since anyone's tried."

The big elf nodded. "Chastity and Kres Renvy are out taking a look. They'll find something." He shifted his attention to the scene behind Myrindi. "This lot seems intent on tearing the walls down with their bare hands. If they try, they're in for a world o' hurt."

"I thought you wanted to get me out of the city."

Lep shrugged. "Pike still does, but he's on enough painkillers to knock out an elephant. Let's just say he's outvoted. Chas *really* wants a shot at the bastards behind the bastards that laid us all up."

An awkward silence descended upon the group. Myrindi knew it was her turn to say something funny or charismatic, but nothing came. She decided to get her intended task over with. "Fro, do you have my diary?"

"Of course, Princess."

So it *had* been Rayn's pinwheel after all, then. Sure, it hurt that her bestie had definitely screwed them, but at least the princess herself hadn't brought Gaptorix to the archives and to Anstrum's door by broadcasting her situation—and her most intimate thoughts—directly to Sorrin. Fro began checking his pockets with his good hand.

"I didn't have you pegged as a diary kind of girl," Sharn said mischievously.

Relieved, Myrindi's sense of humor returned. "I fill it with fantasies about eloping with rich, middle-aged accountants and fast food heirs."

"You're aiming too low. You're a princess. Don't settle for anything less than a slimy old man who owns at least five used car dealerships and stars in all his own commercials."

"Still a step up from the losers my father tried to set me up with."

The look of dread on Fro's face froze them both. "Your diary appears to be missing, Your Highness. I apologize for not taking better care of it."

Myrindi quivered against a sudden chill. "When's the last time you saw it?"

"Back in the storage room, when you told me to keep it safe. I'm sure it's in the palace somewhere."

Deflated, Myrindi leaned against Sharn and put her head in her hands. "Don't worry, Fro. I know exactly where it is."

Dear Diary,

I've decided to turn myself in.

Yeah, I know. That means hanging out with Twat Face Jr. until a very specific, probably sort-of-immediate until-death-do-we-part. Let's face it: dude's not going to want to put up with me for much longer than the nine months it'll take me to give him a daughter he can start peddling to the highest bidder. To walk back into that palace and place myself at Sorrin's mercy is to sign my own death warrant.

Still, I've decided it's worth it. If I let my subjects throw themselves at the palace's defenses I won't have any subjects left. It's an impossible fight. The walls can't be scaled. The portcullis can't be broken. Renvy and Chas checked all the secret tunnels Fro knew of and found them all collapsed. The Glittering Gardens can keep the palace's occupants fed and watered for decades. A siege just isn't practical, especially with a force made up primarily of civilians—regardless of their obvious enthusiasm for the cause.

And there's still a bigger problem, one that of course stems from my princess-ness: the land demands a king, and a king can only be crowned via a wedding ceremony performed inside the throne room. The motherfuckers who built the princess magic way back in the day sure knew how to maintain their hold on Talvayne, huh? Doesn't matter where the princess goes or who she marries; if she gives a shit about the city and its people, she's beholden to whoever controls the palace. Fucking bullshit. I'm a spoiled, stuck-up brat, but I can't just let my subjects fight and die in a losing battle on my behalf. Maybe I could have at least considered it before they saved me from Gaptorix's trolls, but now...fuck, I just can't do it. Nor am I willing to leave them behind to lose their homes to earthquakes and the dissolution of the magic that keeps the different climates separate. And that's without even thinking about what the Rot will eventually do if I flee. This is my city and these are my people and I can't just let it all fall apart. Fuck you, Diary.

So I snuck out of the barracks that had become the headquarters of my revolution. I found the nearest troll—a low-ranking sad sack who'd been left behind by his retreating fellows—and announced both my identity and my intentions. He's bringing me in. I figure I'll be safer with an escort. The city's super tense right now, and I've passed more than a few groups who look like they're up to no good. Plus, my new troll pal will make a great distraction if Fro or any of the others tries to track me down and stop me.

The palace isn't far now. This has been the longest short walk of my entire life, Diary. I know what's waiting for me at the end of it. I'm perfectly willing to cooperate with King Sorrin if it'll make my life even a smidge easier or protect my people. The alternative—buckets of blood running through my streets and effectively across my hands—is too gruesome to consider, even though it means giving the dude who killed my father exactly what he wants. Far better nobles than I have suffered far worse for their people, right? Probably. History's not my strong suit. But anyway, it's my time to show what it really means to be royalty. I just hope the man I'm about to marry is ready to do the same.

— CHAPTER TWELVE —

Sharn caught up to Myrindi and Rittenbrick just a few blocks from the palace. "Princess!" he hissed. "Hold up!"

Myrindi whirled angrily and glared at him from under the hood of her cloak. "Fucking hell!" she snapped. "Why not just call all the neighbors and let them know I'm here?"

He pulled up next to her, clearly out of breath. "Sorry. I've been thinking...you can't go in there alone."

Although that was exactly the sort of sappy bullshit that made her heart fire faster and louder than a machine gun when it came out of Sharn's mouth, Myrindi still rolled her eyes. "We've been over this. I won't be alone. Rittenbrick's going to turn me in and rally whatever trolls are still loyal while I find a way to deal with Sorrin. It'll work."

Sharn wasn't convinced. "What if there aren't any other trolls on our side?"

"There will be others, especially with Gaptorix dead," Rittenbrick rumbled. "That is how our culture works: she who kills the strongest member of the tribe has proven herself to be the true strongest member of the tribe."

Myrindi flashed them a sassy "yeah, that's me, bitches" grin. Sharn crossed his arms. "But what if you get caught?"

"I will not get caught," Rittenbrick replied.

"But what if you do?"

The princess put her hand on the troll's huge arm to stop the argument about to erupt. She'd had enough of this conversation, but she liked Sharn too much to just dismiss him offhand. "If you've got a better idea, let's hear it."

He pointed toward the canvas duffel at Rittenbrick's hip. "Put me in your kit bag."

"You won't fit."

"Actually, he will," Myrindi said happily. She liked where this was going. "Promise me you won't do anything stupid, Sharn."

He closed the space between them and winked. "Don't worry, Your Highness. I'll be right there next to you when you take back your throne."

Myrindi couldn't help herself. She stood up on her tiptoes and gave him a quick peck on the side of his chin. That brief contact sent hot electricity coursing through her nerves and left her aching for more—doubly so when he realized what had just happened and started to blush.

"Open up your kit and put it on the ground," the princess instructed Rittenbrick.

He clearly still didn't get it, but he obeyed anyway. Sharn took his shoes off, put one bare foot atop the clothing and equipment inside the bag, and slowly turned into loose sand.

"See you soon, Princess."

— CHAPTER THIRTEEN —

The trio of trolls at the Gate of Illumination knew exactly what to do when Myrindi arrived.

"Drink this," the leader demanded, pressing a metal flask into her hands.

"What is it?"

"A mild thickener."

Myrindi raised the flask in a mock toast. "To the king." The liquid inside had the consistency of a milkshake and tasted like chalk. She drained it in a single shot. A wave of lethargy swept over her immediately. She couldn't help flashing back to the last time she'd been drugged with a thickener. Her brilliant scheme to remove Sorrin wouldn't work so well if he had her lobotomized as soon as she walked through the front door. She had to trust that he wasn't stupid enough to harm her and bring the wrath of Talvayne's entire population down on his head.

The guards fell into step beside and behind the princess and Rittenbrick as they escorted the pair through the portcullis and into the courtyard. Myrindi was struck by how normal it all looked. An imposter king who'd murdered her father sat upon the throne, and yet the grass was still green, the mortar in the brick path leading to the palace was still impossibly white, and the exterior of the keep still glistened in the warm sun. Sure, it smelled kind of funky because of the pile of dead kings on the far side of the palace, but that seemed natural and normal, too. The land ached for a king and the people fought for a princess, but most of Talvayne just didn't give a shit whose ass was planted on which fancy chair. Myrindi wondered what had become of her father's prized carriage and unicorns. She assumed they were safe and sound and as stupid as ever.

"So, how's life under King Sorrin?" the princess asked the guards. Thanks to the thickener, her words came out a little too slowly to achieve the air of cockiness she wanted. "Everything turning out bright and rosy and wonderful for all of trollkind?"

They pretended to ignore her. The troll to her left—slightly shorter than the others, with a mangled hole where his nose should've been—shifted his shoulders uncomfortably.

"I thought not. Who's running the troll side of this little conspiracy now that Gaptorix is gone?"

No Nose glanced down at her suspiciously. "What happened to Gaptorix?"

"You haven't heard?" She paused a moment for dramatic effect. "Oh, of course you haven't. Sorrin wouldn't want this to spread. Gaptorix got fresh with me and I killed the bastard."

The troll to her right burst out laughing, a sound like an old refrigerator sputtering to life. "Nice try, Your Highness."

"It is true," Rittenbrick said solemnly. "I have seen the body."

"A fake," Righty protested, but not confidently.

"Drowned the big lug myself," Myrindi added. "That makes me your chieftain or mayor or CEO or something, right?"

No one answered. No Nose eyed the princess with what she assumed was grudging respect, then looked away to study his feet instead. Myrindi's lips twisted into a smirk. Mission accomplished.

Tall and bulbous and made of ruby carved to look like a blazing sun, the keep's main doors swung slowly open as the group approached. Four more trolls awaited them in the small anteroom inside. They fell into lock step around and in front of the princess' entourage and together they all climbed the five-step staircase up to the Lambent Path.

"Hi there, loyal guards!" Myrindi tried to chirp through her dry, cracked throat. "Everybody having a nice day? Gosh, it sure is nice of King Sorrin to send you all to get me! It's not like I've made this walk a million times before or anything. Unless...he's not *afraid* of me, is he? You know, because I killed Gaptorix?"

One of the new trolls glowered back at her briefly, but the others didn't acknowledge her. She decided to leave it alone, mostly because her voice was starting to falter because of the thickener and she knew she was going to need it to deal with Sorrin. Rolling over and playing dead wouldn't work; it had to be a negotiation tinged with the threat of a verbal blitzkrieg. She'd made it plain in her diary what she thought of him, so a total reversal would make him suspicious. The princess had to bill her surrender as a sacrifice—one she hated more than anything but the thought of letting her people die in what would be a vain attempt to recapture the castle. The truth of that would shine through easily enough if she let it.

They found Sorrin lounging lazily atop the Throne of Light, his legs dangling across one of the arm rests. He looked like a small child sitting in daddy's giant recliner. The Staff of Forinex rested in his lap and a golden crown sat atop his leafy hair at a jaunty angle. Beside the throne stood an older, more weathered version of Sorrin—his father.

"Twat Face and Twat Face Jr.," Myrindi muttered. "Lovely."

Sorrin's father raised his hand to stop the princess and her entourage when they were perhaps halfway across the throne room. "That is close enough. Princess Myrindi, please allow me the privilege of introducing King Sorrin, First of His Name, Ruler of Talvayne and Defender of the Realm."

"Yo," Myrindi said.

"That's all you have to say for yourself?" Sorrin replied disinterestedly.

She shrugged. "Seemed like an all right place to start. We've got a lot to talk about, you and I."

"Do we really? It would seem to me that you strolled into my lair undefended and with nothing even remotely resembling leverage."

"Not true. I've got a whole city's worth of leverage behind me. Harm me, and...well...they won't breach the palace walls immediately. You'll probably have at least a small chance of escaping to live a fulfilling life on the run with zero power and even less influence. But the people will get in here eventually, and it will take a lot more than some fancy magic stick and a few trolls to stop them all."

"Why not just bide your time, then? Wait for the people to hurl themselves at my walls like fleshy missiles until they find a way through?"

"Because I can't let that many die for me. Because Talvayne probably doesn't have enough time. The land needs a king, Sorrin, and I'm not sure it'll get one before this place shakes itself to pieces unless you and I put aside our differences and do what's best for *our* people."

The wood nymph paused, considering that, then reached behind his leg and held up a small leather book: Myrindi's diary. The princess remembered to drop her jaw and widen her eyes in mock surprise as planned even though she couldn't believe he was arrogant enough to reveal his hand so early. He tossed the little book toward her. It landed a few feet short.

"So what you wrote is true, then. You've had a change of heart. You've grown up. You love *the people*." Disdain practically dripped from Sorrin's tongue. "And yet you hate me."

She decided to roll with it. "Of course I do. Without once asking for my input, my father decided you would be the only man I would ever be allowed to have anything even remotely resembling a relationship with. You expect me to just bat my eyes and swoon and accept you? That ain't how it works, pal."

"Yes, it is. You are a Talvayan Crown Princess. That is how it's always fucking worked."

Myrindi recoiled in both horror and disgust. Although she'd lived with that truth for as long as she could remember, hearing it spoken so plainly still stung. "You know I'm a person, right?"

Sorrin drummed his fingers on the throne's armrest. "I know that discussing this with you is like debating the merits of a steak dinner with a cow. Here's the deal: we're getting married tonight, we're consummating the union soon after, and if there's anything good left in this world you will be out of my hair in nine short months. You're going to cooperate fully or I'm going to pull out a few of your fingernails. I'm in a generous mood, so I'll give your co-conspirators forty-eight hours to get the hell out of my city. After that, they'll be killed on sight. You'll be allowed to fulfill your role as queen and make all the requisite appearances, but you will have zero influence on my reign and you will keep your pretty little mouth shut when you're around me. Got all that?"

Myrindi didn't respond.

"Well?" Sorrin asked angrily after a few moments of awkward silence.

She shrugged and batted her eyes innocently.

The wood nymph sighed. "You can speak when spoken to, smartass."

The princess let out a deep breath, feigning relief. "If that's all you need...sure, let's do it."

Sorrin frowned. The heavy sigh he unleashed probably would've knocked his father over if the man had been standing closer. "Whatever. Guards, confine the princess to her quarters before she pulls whatever dumb stunt she's planning. I'll see you later this evening, my love."

Dear Diary,

First off, don't worry. You've been safely hidden. Second, Rayn was waiting for me when I got to my chambers.

"What's up, traitor?" I said as I strolled into my bedroom. The place was a mess. Sorrin's thugs had torn through everything looking for Rot knows what. All the clothes from my walk-in closet and dresser drawers had been strewn across the floor. They'd punched holes in the walls and the ceiling. And when I find the jerk who took a knife to my mattress, that asshole's on unicorn shit shoveling duty until the day he fucking dies.

"I expected that," Rayn replied. She sat at the foot of the bed with her hands clasped in her lap like some wholesome sitcom mother preparing to impart the hokey wisdom of the world to a daughter who'd gotten caught smoking at the bus stop. "I expected that," she repeated when I didn't respond, "but I don't deserve it."

I crossed my arms and leaned back against the wall beside a jagged crater where my favorite mirror used to be. It was on the floor nearby in about 500 pieces. "Oh, this I've got to hear."

She adjusted her dress and shifted her weight on what was left of my mattress. "Do you know what it is I do, Myrindi?"

"Yes. You fuck with people. You lead them on and you lead them on and then you stab them in the back." Lingering dust from the demolition of my chambers brought tears to my eyes.

"In a manner of speaking, yes." She took a deep breath. "I put the right people into the proper positions so they can enact the sorts of drastic changes needed to make the world a much better place."

"Sure you do. King Sorrin's definitely a huge improvement on the status quo. It's no wonder they call you the Witch."

Rayn visibly flinched. I've never seen her show anything even remotely resembling vulnerability. The surprising awkwardness of the motion convinced me it wasn't an act. "That ignorant sapling is just a means to an end," she replied. "He's an obstacle I set up for you to overcome in such a way as to affirm your position atop Talvayne's new sociopolitical landscape."

"The fuck does that even mean?"

"It means when you win, you are absolutely in charge. Think about it, Myrindi: he usurped the throne and killed all the kings except his father and Froman. Not only is he the greatest villain this town's seen since Axzar dropped the drizzling shits that turned into the Rot, he's done all the dirty work necessary to provide Talvayne's next ruler with an immediate mandate to invoke sweeping changes without *any* opposition. So when *you* take that bastard down in front of the whole city, what happens?"

My jaw dropped. It was the craziest thing I'd heard since that one time my father suggested he might hire a Royal Nutritionist. And yet it made a certain amount of sense. It fit Rayn's style. It was brilliant in its ballsy insanity, beautiful in its chaotic logic, and terrifying because holy shit it put a ton on my shoulders. "I'd be able to pick the father of my daughter," I muttered. "I'd be able to stop the buying and selling of princesses."

She nodded and clapped her hands excitedly, returning to her old self. "Exactly."

But I wasn't completely buying it. "And what about that pinwheel? What was that about?"

"It summoned me. It meant you were in trouble and it was time for me to get my butt back to Talvayne."

"But...you didn't show. You were late."

Rayn shook her head. "No. I was there. I watched from the mists adjacent to Anstrum's land. That bitchy old wisp *really* needs to hire a decorator."

I dropped my hands and balled them into angry fists. "Why the fuck didn't you help me? Do you have *any* idea how fucking disgusting the respiratory system of a fucking troll is? Rot, I can still smell the big loser all over me."

"If I had swooped in and rescued you in front of all your subjects...how would that have looked? Would they have rallied to you the same way?"

"I guess not," I growled.

"Exactly. You've got Talvayne in the palm of your hand right now, Myrindi. All that's left to do is remove Sorrin and take the throne."

She was right. I couldn't argue with her logic, as much as I hated all the drama it had put me through. Rayn had done a lot for me, but the way she'd done it just didn't feel good. I'm just a piece in the convoluted chessboard floating through her twisted mind—an important piece, and one she kind of likes, but a piece nonetheless.

"What if I can't do it?" I asked.

"Stop that. You absolutely *can*." She paused. "But if for some reason you *don't*, then I'll have to reevaluate and move on to my next plan. And I'll have been wrong."

I cocked one eyebrow. "How often does that happen?"

"It's rare, but when it happens it really, really sucks." She cocked her head and smiled sadly. "I'll be there for your daughter either way."

That one was like a kick to the gut, but it got her point across. This wasn't just about me or Sorrin or the people of Talvayne anymore. It was about diverting the course of history, of finally making a change that probably never would've happened without Rayn's intervention.

But at what cost? The Conclave of Kings was decimated. My father was dead. Talvayne was embroiled in a bitter civil war. Sure, the kings were a bunch of twats and probably got exactly what they deserved, but they were still living, breathing people. I guess. And what of those who'd fought and died in the streets, swept up by the madness of the moment and a cause they may not have fully grasped? Rayn had obviously done the math and decided it was all worth it—assuming I come through, of course. Although I could process her cold logic, I couldn't really relate to it. I couldn't help wondering what had happened to her that made her brain work that way. I mean, I've had a pretty shitty life, but I never wanted to kill anybody as a means of getting out of it.

I reminded myself that Sharn was still out there, carefully examining the situation and zeroing in on the appropriate solution. He'd get the job done, and then he and I could live happily ever after.

But still. The dust in the room was just too much. Tears streamed down my face. A blast of heavy raindrops splattered against the windows as a storm whipped into action. "Will you be at the wedding?" I asked. "I could use a maid of honor. Or someone to walk me down the aisle. Or a flower girl. Or whatever you want, really."

Rayn shook her head. "I appreciate the invitation, but I must respectfully decline. This part's on you, love." My mother's old ivory hairbrush, casually tossed on the floor by some asshole troll, zipped through the air and into my bestie's hand. "But I'll do your hair."

I scooted over to the bed and sat down with my back to Rayn. We were close enough that I could feel her breath on the back of my neck, but I couldn't make myself look at her. "Don't mess it up," I croaked. "It's a big day. A girl only gets one first wedding."

— CHAPTER FOURTEEN —

Myrindi was trying on her fifth wedding dress option—a frilly white sheath she'd once worn to a formal ball celebrating the completion of a bridge or something—when the soft chime signaling a visitor awaiting admittance to the princess's chambers rang. Pippa, the only servant Sorrin had assigned to Myrindi, politely excused herself from her zipper zipping and fashion critiquing duties and left the bedroom to answer the bell. That Pippa had unwittingly delivered the mojito spiked with thickener that set up Dr. Neltsin's failed lobotomy attempt was not lost on the princess. Sorrin had sent the short water nymph as a reminder of how brutal he could be if he didn't get his way. In response, Myrindi had decided to treat Pippa as her new best friend. They'd cleaned the bedroom together, shared a meal of grilled cheese and tomato soup, gossiped about the boys who worked in the palace, laughed and held each other during the increasingly frequent earthquakes, and generally turned what should've been a really awkward situation into a super fun sleepover.

Pippa was particularly impressed with Myrindi's hair, which Rayn had somehow braided into a complex, looping pretzel with no obvious beginning or end. "I did it myself," Myrindi had lied. It bothered her that she couldn't even give Rayn credit for something as simple as a hairstyle, but such was the life her bestie had chosen. Rayn claimed she didn't mind, but Myrindi suspected that wasn't completely true. She knew the Witch better than anyone, and she didn't miss the ever so slight quiver in Rayn's voice whenever the subject was broached.

Pippa returned with a perfectly wrapped gift box cradled in her arms. "Someone left this outside the door," she said. "There's no tag and no sign of whoever brought it."

Myrindi's heart leapt into her throat. Sharn! It had to be from Sharn. Sorrin had made a huge mistake not posting any guards directly outside her chambers, and the sand nymph had made him pay for it by delivering some sort of ward, charm, or weapon that would turn the tables on their little wooden nemesis. Never mind where he'd found the sparkly yellow paper and the big purple bow. Sharn was smart. Sharn was resourceful. Sharn could really wrap the shit out of a present. He could do anything, and Myrindi couldn't wait to see what he would do next.

Pippa placed the box on the princess's shredded mattress. She'd barely let go before Myrindi pounced upon it and and tore the paper away as if it were one of Sharn's tight T-shirts. The princess lifted the exposed lid away with a bright smile and peered inside.

"Oh," she growled, slumping back in defeat. In the distance, thunder rumbled. "Motherfucker."

Pippa leaned around the princess to get a look. "Oh, Rot!" she shrieked, spinning away and clutching her mouth as if she were about to vomit. "You know who that...belonged to?"

Myrindi gently put the lid back on the box. "Yup," she snarled. Salty tears streamed down her face. "That's Sharn's head."

Dear Diary,

Forgive me if any of this comes out screwier than usual. I'm on enough painkillers right now to knock out an entire heavy metal band. I swear my knee's the size of a damn watermelon. I can't really see so well out of my left eye. It's going to be a few weeks until my next dance party, to say the least. I'm probably never going to walk quite right ever again without some serious magical intervention. Maybe I'll leave it that way for the street cred.

Rittenbrick and the other three trolls that had escorted me into the palace came for me at sundown. I met them in my parlor.

"King Sorrin's not going to like this," the leader said. No Nose tried to hide a smile.

"Getting married in workout clothes is super trendy in London right now," I replied. "*Everybody* who's *anybody* is skipping the dress and going nontraditional."

I'd borrowed a pair of pink gym shorts, a black T-shirt, and a pair of white tennis shoes from Pippa. My fists and wrists were wrapped in white athletic tape. The outfit totally didn't go with my hair, but whatever. A touch of elegance never hurts.

Rittenbrick stepped forward and bowed his head. "Your Highness, a private word about the evening's festivities?"

"Of course." I dismissed the other three with an arrogant wave of my hand. Rittenbrick and I took a few steps back toward my bedroom.

"Sup?" I whispered.

"The majority of the guard is behind you," he said softly. "All they need is a push. Something to set them off and make them act."

I smiled up at the big lug and patted his beefy bicep affectionately. Rittenbrick had just given me all I needed to know I was on the right track. The nagging doubts that had haunted the back of my mind since I'd first whipped up my plan evaporated. "Count on it, dude. Also...ah...what's with the loincloths?" All four of the trolls had rolled into my chambers dressed like Gaptorix. It was a bit unsettling.

Rittenbrick blushed. "Traditional troll formal wear."

"Huh," I replied, genuinely surprised. "I never knew that." Turns out Gaptorix had actually been the best-dressed person in the room all along.

We took the long way to the throne room, looping around the outer edge of the keep via a narrow, little-used hallway that eventually bisected the Lambent Path. On sunny days, the dusty corridor's stained glass windows would've twinkled with a million different colors, but it was my wedding day and I was pissed so the whole thing was just kind of dull. Those windows gave me a great view of the dead kings rotting away on that side of the courtyard, though, which I guess was the point of that route.

"I am not happy about the state of my lawn," I snarled to no one in particular. "This is a big fucking day and my hubby-to-be can't even be bothered to pick up his toys? *Not* okay."

No Nose snorted. I decided I kind of liked that guy. The others pretended to ignore me.

An organ roared into a light, airy tune as we stepped onto the Lambent Path. One of the palace's longest tenured servants, a graying female lycan whose name I've never been able to remember, gave my outfit the stink eye and handed me a bouquet of blue glitteroses.

"Got a problem?" I snapped as I snatched away the flowers and hurled them against the wall in one smooth motion. The flimsy flowers exploded in a burst of pretty petals—the perfect metaphor for my upcoming wedding.

The lycan flinched and took a step back. "N-no, Your Highness," she replied, quickly bowing her head.

"Speak freely," I demanded. "This is my wedding day and I only get one. If something about it isn't perfect, I want to know."

She looked me up and down one more time, glanced nervously at the guards, and finally shrugged. "A big, frilly gown would've given you more places to hide some weapons, Your Highness."

I burst out laughing. No Nose snickered. "I like the way you think," I said happily. "I'm doubling your salary."

The lycan smiled, baring her sharp fangs. "Thank you, Your Highness. I wish you luck today."

I nodded and started down the Lambent Path. Rittenbrick and the others fell into step behind me, leaving just enough space between us to make it kind of look like I wasn't being herded into a wedding ceremony I didn't actually want. The obnoxious organ music set my blood boiling even hotter. I glared fiery death at every stupid old king's statue I passed. Those greedy, evil fucks were the ultimate reason for my current predicament and—if I'm being brutally honest here—my entire shitty existence. I fantasized about stabbing each of them in the face and then hosting a super fun brunch with a make-your-own Bloody Mary bar for all the princesses they'd bought and sold and essentially murdered.

"Fuck you all," I whispered. "Never again."

A pair of yellow pixies pulled the throne room's double doors open as I approached. The organist crashed through a rather appropriate crescendo that reminded me of the start of a thunderstorm. As is customary at Talvayan royal weddings, guests stood and watched from two huge crowds separated by a wide aisle leading to the dais and the Throne of Light, where the groom and the king performing the ceremony awaited the bride's arrival. The princess, thanks to her life as an over-protected shut-in, doesn't get a "side" in the traditional sense; guests are typically movers and shakers in Talvayne's upper crust, people with reputations or power or status with whom the new king would like to curry favor. In this case, that meant a shitload of wood nymphs in bright robes and stupidly tall hats, a few clusters of bright wisps, and a small smattering of the other races. Several dozen troll guards in loincloths stood watch around the perimeter.

The scene was set for a perfectly traditional royal wedding—at least until I walked in. The distressed murmur that spread as people caught sight of me certainly was not customary. My choice of outfits rocked the throne room harder than any of the day's increasingly common earthquakes. Even several of the guards broke protocol to add to the whispers. Royal wedding gowns are typically elaborate, complex affairs that influence Talvayan fashion for years. My mother, for instance, spawned a poofy shoulder pad trend that was the scourge of formal parties until sometime around my seventh birthday. I smiled evilly at the thought of all the vapid socialites about to run out and buy dozens of pairs of gym shorts and running sneakers.

Clad in matching gold togas with green trim, Sorrin and his father gaped at me from the dais with "oh my god, who fucking farted?" expressions of disbelief. The pretender also wore a crown carefully tilted atop his stupid head at an angle that achieved maximum doucheness. I'd strutted across about half of the throne room when Sorrin waved his hands angrily to silence the crowd and the annoying music. I kind of wanted to thank him for the latter.

"Princess Myrindi!" he tried to bellow. It came out a bit squeaky. "This is a wedding, not a Zumba class! You will not take another step forward until you explain your attire to the guests and the fiancé so you've so callously offended!"

I stopped as instructed. "I declare this proposed union illegal, dishonorable, and unwanted. It would bring shame upon my person and my family," I said clearly and confidently. "I demand raktarr, the sacred rite of trial by virtuous combat."

The guests gasped. The trolls hooted and cheered. Sorrin looked at me like I'd just told him his mother was a bicycle. "You are not a troll," he replied when the din died down, "and their laws and rituals hold no influence within these walls."

It was exactly the wrong thing to say. Twat Face Jr. had just rejected one of the most hallowed traditions of his power base: a bride's right to challenge a groom she finds unworthy. The guards howled in protest for a few seconds, but then their animalistic wailing was slowly replaced by a steady chant: "Raktarr! Raktarr! Raktarr!"

I hopped up and down and threw a few practice punches, buoyed by adrenaline and the knowledge that I'd just cornered my opponent. Denying raktarr and attempting to force the wedding would turn Sorrin's only true leverage—his trolls—against him. Only a spineless, salad eating, honor-less worm turns down such a challenge. After I had finished bawling over what happened to Sharn, Pippa and I read up on our troll traditions and came up with one hell of a plan. That girl's also getting a raise. And maybe some of the uglier jewelry from the royal collection.

Sorrin and his father exchanged nervous glances. Both knew the would-be king couldn't say no.

"What's the matter?" I shouted. "Afraid to fight a teenage girl?"

That drove the trolls into a frenzy of clapping and stomping and chanting. I swear the entire keep shook. Guess it could've been an earthquake, but it felt different. More rhythmic and regular. Less angry.

"Fine!" Sorrin snarled. The trolls roared. "Raktarr it is!"

He handed his crown to his father and stomped down from the dais with absolute murder in his eyes. A dozen or so trolls pushed their way through the shocked audience to form a ring around the two of us. Rittenbrick and my three other guards closed the circle behind me. No Nose flashed me a sassy wink.

I'd gotten Sorrin exactly where I wanted him. We were about even in weight, but I had the reach advantage and a secret weapon: the water. If I could grab hold of his and yank it out of him the way I'd pulled the tap water back in Dr. Neltsin's office, I could end the fight before he got in even a single shot. It's an old water nymph trick, one I probably should've familiarized myself with a long time ago, but who needs crap like that when you've got a Fro and a Rayn watching your back? I'd practiced with Pippa earlier and sent the poor girl running to her quarters in tears. Double raise. And maybe one or two pretty pieces of jewelry.

I closed my eyes and reached out for Sorrin's water. I couldn't find it. There was too much of the stuff in the room given the size of the crowd. I probably should've thought of that, but what can you do? I wasn't all that concerned about it. Sorrin's a puss, right? I assumed we'd end up in the sort of rolling-around-on-the floor slappy fight that would eventually help me zero in on his particular brand of rotten H2O.

When I opened my eyes, Sorrin was warming up with a flurry of precise punches and a Jackie Chan-level roundhouse kick. "Son of a bitch," I muttered. So Sorrin's a puss trained in martial arts. Plan B—if I needed it—was really going to hurt.

I glanced at the troll to my left, a pug-nosed brute with a skull tattooed on his bulbous gut. "Do the honors, please."

He bowed reverently, then raised his fist. All of the other trolls immediately went silent and totally freaked out the non-troll wedding guests. "Raktarr is not settled until one side yields or dies. Do you both understand?"

Sorrin and I nodded in turn.

The troll brought his meaty fist down to smack his open palm. "Raktarr!" he bellowed.

The crowd exploded. Shrieking wood nymphs and whistling wisps and who knows what else joined with the deep voices of the trolls to create a wild sound that put the organist to shame. It was exhilarating.

Sorrin sauntered across the floor with his arms hanging limp at his sides. "First shot's yours, Princess," he snarled. "Better make it count."

"Yield," I snapped. "Yield or you will die."

He laughed. "Not before the honeymoon, sweetie. Hope you realize just how hard you've made things for your—"

I slammed my open palm into the bridge of his pointy little nose before he could finish. The crackling sensation of cartilage or wood or whatever was in there coming apart in my hand might be the most satisfying thing I've ever felt. Sorrin stumbled backward with a yelp, clutching desperately at his face. Blood the color and consistency of maple syrup oozed out from between his fingers and spattered all over his stupid toga.

The crowd erupted as I rushed the reeling wood nymph. He stepped aside and expertly swept my legs out from under me. The back of my head crashed into the hard stone with a gross crack. Pain shot through every nerve in my body. My vision went black for a few heartbeats and then treated me to a lovely spinning view of the ceiling when it decided to come back. I didn't get to enjoy it for long; Sorrin stomped down hard on my knee and blew it all apart. Only my agonized scream drowned out the sound of snapping bone and sinew. The onlookers booed lustily, but their disdain for my opponent was little consolation as I writhed and sobbed on the floor.

"Do you yield, Princess?" Sorrin asked.

"Never!" I shrieked, choking back a sob. "Do you?"

Some of the spectators laughed at me, but more of them cheered. Sorrin drove his foot into my side and knocked all the air out of my lungs.

"Yield!" he demanded.

"Kiss my skinny blue ass!" I gasped. The gills in my neck flared painfully as my body fought for breath.

He kicked me again and again and again. My lower ribs shattered. I coughed up blood in between sobs and screams. By the time he stopped I'd lost track of the blows. My leg, side, and head were on fire. I could barely breathe. I've never felt so shitty.

I rolled away from Sorrin to try to protect my injuries even though doing so really fucking hurt. He didn't follow up his previous attack. He thought he was giving me time to think about what he had just done to me, but what he really gave me was a chance to focus and steel myself to implement plan B, the second old troll tradition I'd brought with me to my wedding, my nuclear option: a request for an immediate and honorable death. Perhaps the one rite the trolls hold more sacred than raktarr. Any individual who refuses to grant it faces immediate exile—or execution at the hands of the community. That's right, Diary: I'd decided to bet my life that Sorrin would prefer living on the run to either his own death or the effective end of Talvayne. Killing me meant no means of crowning a legitimate king and ending the earthquakes—if the Rot didn't wash over it all first. Denying my request and refusing to leave would be the immediate end of him at the hands of the surrounding trolls.

My breath caught in my throat as I coughed out the awkward trollish word. "Pahlung," I choked out, spitting blood all over the floor. My voice was raspy and ragged. No one heard me—or if they did, they couldn't determine what I'd said. "Pahlung," I tried again with roughly the same effect.

The crowd quieted. Sorrin stepped over me and knelt down close. "What was that, Princess? Do you yield?"

I was about to repeat myself when something warm and wet dripped down onto my cheek: Sorrin's blood. A rush of heat coursed through my body. I could feel his water. I definitely preferred the idea of thoroughly beating Sorrin to just winning on a technicality. Or you know, dying. I reached out for Twat Face Jr.'s water, took firm hold, and yanked.

The bastard went rigid, his eyes wide and his jaw slack. The crowd gasped as water bubbled out of his eyes, his mouth, his nose, his ears—and, yeah, his other orifices. All of it trickled and spattered down onto yours truly. He convulsed as if being electrocuted as his flesh fought to hold onto the liquid it needed to survive. He choked raggedly, fighting the fluid building up in his throat as he tried desperately to breathe and, probably, to yield. I wasn't going to let him do either. Not after all he'd done to me and my family and my friends and my fucking city. No way. Sorrin hadn't asked for an honorable death, but I gave him one anyway.

Dried to a gray husk, Sorrin toppled to his left and hit the floor with a sharp crack. I lay in a puddle of his body's water, letting my gills revel in the wet goodness and not giving a shit that doing so was actually kind of gross. A mighty cheer rose up from most of those gathered in the throne room as Sorrin's family fled the scene.

I won. Talvayne and its people are mine.

— CHAPTER FIFTEEN —

R ot, really?" Myrindi snapped from the Throne of Light.
Another earthquake shook the palace. "What else you
got, Pippa?"

The latest applicant for Talvayne's vacant king position—a
tall, thin sand nymph in a crisp black suit—took a step toward
the dais and spread his hands wide in confusion. "But, Your
Highness, the connections I've forged among the social and
business elite of Talvayne make me—"

"—a giant douche," the princess said. Rittenbrick and No
Nose, standing guard to either side of Myrindi, snickered. Kres
Renvy rolled his eyes.

"He does rather resemble a feminine hygiene product," Chas
added. She and Lep sat at the foot of the dais, a picnic lunch of
sandwiches and fruit and a bottle of wine spread out between
them. The big elf smiled and rubbed his wife's shoulder.

The sand nymph ran a hand through his short black hair,
clearly fighting to maintain his composure. "I will be a just and
merciful king. And I will give you a beautiful daughter."

Myrindi leaned across the throne and poked Pippa in the elbow. "See, that's the problem right there. None of these dudes get it."

Pippa and Fro looked back at her in confusion. "I'm...not quite sure I get it either, Your Highness," Pippa said.

Before the princess could explain, Pike decided to join the conversation. "It's simple: everything these jerks want contradicts Her Princessness's royal goals, of which there are at least two. Number one: she wants to be in charge. Number two: she doesn't want some asshole signing her death warrant by knocking her up." He'd taken a seat against the wall to the left of the throne, beside the thirty-rack of cheap beer he'd asked for as an advance on payment for services rendered. About a dozen empty, crushed cans surrounded him. Myrindi had never seen him so happy.

"But...bearing a child and securing Talvayne for the next generation is the queen's most sacred duty!" the sand nymph protested.

"You should probably leave before she asks her trolls to break your arms," Pike slurred.

The sand nymph's milky white eyes darted from Myrindi to Rittenbrick to No Nose, and then he spun on his heel and ran for the exit.

"Former Council of War Pike," Lep muttered. "Master of throne room politics."

The elf's discarded cans rattled across the floor as another short earthquake struck. Fro stepped around Pippa to catch Myrindi's attention. "Princess, I understand your desire to find a proper mate, but we can't allow these tremors to continue. The city will tear itself apart if a king is not found."

Myrindi sighed and leaned back in her seat. She understood the situation and it was starting to wear on her. Every hour she delayed the inevitable meant more earthquakes, more unrest, and potentially more injuries and deaths. The thing she really wanted—that fairytale wedding to the perfect guy who'd stood by her through thick and thin—had died with Sharn. She wasn't immature enough to think he was the only man she'd ever love, but finding that sort of relationship required time Talvayne simply didn't have. A compromise was the city's only hope.

All that said, Myrindi couldn't bear the thought of installing another king who wanted to keep things as fucked up as they'd always been—not after everything she and her friends and Talvayne itself had been through. It felt like an insult to everyone who'd fought for her. Rayn had rigged the board so Myrindi could change the game, and there was no way she was going to pass up the opportunity to make things better for all the princesses yet to come.

She closed her eyes and rubbed her forehead, thinking things through. It would've been easier if she weren't so hopped up on painkillers. Finding a legitimate partner for her plan just wasn't an option anymore. So what did that leave? Her mind drifted to the human royalty she'd read about in magazines and on TV. They were mostly figureheads, important by blood and tradition but mostly beholden to the decisions of other governmental bodies. That's what she needed: a king in name only. An employee of sorts. A man who would enjoy the benefits of the position but stay the hell out of her way as she made her ideas into law. Someone with no desire for power because he'd already tasted it and found it far too sour for his liking. Someone who understood what she was about. Someone who wouldn't touch her with a ten-foot pole if she were the last woman on earth.

"The fuck you looking at me like that for?" Pike slurred.

Dear Diary,

—⟨●⟩—

READ ON FOR A SNEAK PEAK OF THE FIRST CHAPTER OF *STRANGER THAN FICTION*, BOOK 4 OF THE DEVIANT MAGIC SERIES.

—⟨●⟩—

— PROLOGUE —

*Excerpt from Chapter 47 of Lazarus Jones
and the Lightning Club: Final Showdown*

You are done for."

Headmaster Aldern—smoking, bloody, his body still spasming with the aftershocks of magical lightning—collapsed to the dirty stone floor and didn't get back up. A ragged gasp squeaked out through his chapped lips.

Kron the Withered leered down at his fallen opponent and cackled. His twisted, emaciated body quivered evilly beneath uncounted layers of tattered gray and black robes.

"Well," Lazzy said to the Lightning Club, "that's not good."

Dash leaned past his friend to peer around the corner of the tunnel leading into Kron's cavernous lair. "Yeah. This is definitely not part of the plan."

Keighlan grabbed them both by the high collars of their school uniforms and yanked them back into hiding. "We have to retreat," she said sternly. Beside her, Gearix adjusted her thick glasses and nodded in meek agreement.

Dash stuck his head back out as soon as Keighlan released her grip. "What's he taking from the headmaster?"

Kron reached into Aldern's robes and tore an amulet from the headmaster's neck. The wrinkled sorcerer stared at his prize with hungry eyes. "Thank you for delivering this to me, brother. With its power I can finally free the archdemon!"

"No way!" Dash hissed. "Kron's the headmaster's brother!"

Lazzy, peering around the corner with his friend once more, shook his head sadly. "That amulet..."

Keighlan pulled them back again. "Seriously guys, it's time to go!" Gearix repeated her previous nod.

But Lazzy wasn't listening. Resolve burning hot in his chest, he stood up straight and buttoned his jacket.

"I know that look," Dash said with a cocky smile.

"We're not going anywhere!" Lazzy declared. His bright blue eyes turned to steel. "We solved the troll's riddle. We tracked down the warlock's diary. We escaped Balacath's trap and killed the hellhound. We put all the clues together and found Kron the Withered's lair behind the blackboard of our Advanced Hex Removal classroom, defeated Balacath once and for all, and tricked Headmaster Aldern into coming here to face Kron for us. We can't run." He surveyed his friends, all of whom stared up at him in awe. "This is our responsibility. We will face Kron the Withered—and we will win!"

Gearix leapt to her feet and pumped her tiny fist. "Yeah!"

Dash stood. "Let's get 'em, Laz."

Keighlan remained seated. "How, exactly, are we going to do that?"

Lazzy smiled. "With a power Kron has never possessed and will never understand." He offered Keighlan his hand. "Help me, K."

She frowned. "I don't know about this..."

"Enough!" Kron's terrible voice boomed through the tight space. "Come out here and let me get a look at you."

The Lightning Club froze. Gearix's lower lip began to quiver. Dash peed a little.

Lazzy was the first to regain his composure. "Come on. If he wants us, he's got us."

One by one they rounded the corner and stepped into Kron's cavernous lair. Lazzy, the handsome young hero with the heart of gold. Gearix, freckled and lanky and nervous. Dash, Lazzy's cocksure best friend. And Keighlan, the beauty and the brains of the Lightning Club's whole operation. This was it: their moment, their big showdown, the confrontation they'd been working toward since they first deciphered the weird runes that kept appearing on their homeroom's blackboard.

They weren't ready. Three of them knew it. The fourth, well...

"You're not getting away with this, Kron!" Lazzy shouted.

The twisted old man cackled. He clutched the amulet in his bony fingers like it was the only thing in the world that mattered. At his feet, Aldern gasped for breath. "Kids. Run."

Lazzy snatched Keighlan's hand in his own and took a defiant step forward. "No. We're not leaving. Kron, return the medallion and turn yourself in!"

"Or what?" Kron asked, his voice tinged with genuine curiosity.

"Or you're the one who's done for!"

The ancient sorcerer rolled his rheumy eyes. "And how exactly are you going to make that come to pass?"

Lazzy tried to take another step toward Kron but Keighlan held him back. "I did a service for the fairy queen," Lazzy replied, undeterred, "and in return she granted me this blessing: as long as she who loves me most is by my side, evil shall do me no harm!"

Kron's malicious yellow smile made them all flinch. "Is that so?"

"Yes!" Lazzy shouted. "Keighlan and I love each other! You have no power over us, you evil bastard!"

Kron laughed again. "Looks to me like the girl might have a little something to say about that."

Beside Lazzy, Keighlan was shaking. The others had never seen her look so small and vulnerable. It sunk their spirits. She closed her eyes and bowed her head.

"K," Lazzy said softly, "what's wrong?"

Keighlan's face flushed and tears streamed down her cheeks. "Damn it, Lazarus!" she snapped. "I don't love you!"

Those four simple words, stated so bluntly and so angrily, tore a ragged hole deep in Lazzy's chest. "That's nonsense!" He blinked at her in disbelief. "What about that night we shared my sleeping bag in the Foreboding Woods?"

"Gnomes stole my pack and it was cold out."

"Or when we got drunk on azacea at the fairy queen's reception and I carried you back to your room?"

She shrugged. "Thanks?"

"Or when I broke Balacath's spell over you at the spring formal, and we slow danced until the chaperones made us go home?"

She cringed away from him. "I'm sorry. I was so relieved to be free of Balacath, and I knew Dash would never ask me to dance, so..."

Lazzy let his grip on Keighlan's hand go slack. For a moment she stared down at the space where his fingers had been, then she darted over to Dash and buried her head in his chest. He hesitantly wrapped an arm around her shoulders and shot his best friend a look of utter shock.

"That's it, then," Lazarus Jones croaked. The confident boy seemed to deflate, his heart well and truly broken—and their one chance to stand up to Kron shattered along with it. Lazzy's obsession with Keighlan and his inability to interpret their friendship as just that had doomed them all. He felt like such a fool.

Pyres of purple energy burst to life in Kron the Withered's hands. "That's enough teenage angst for one day. You did well to make it this far, Lazarus Jones, but your story goes no further."

The Lightning Club steeled themselves for the end. If this was truly it, at least they'd get to go out together. Lazzy and Dash exchanged a brotherly nod, the girl who'd briefly but spectacularly come between them forgotten. Keighlan clutched Dash as tight as she could. Gearix, desperate to reach Lazzy, tripped over her own big feet. He caught her—barely—and pulled her up straight.

"Lazzy," Gearix whispered, her green eyes glistening and twice their normal size, "I love you."

Kron clapped his hands together and sent a blast of violet death spiraling toward the Lightning Club. It struck Lazzy and Gearix first...

...and bounced right back, reflected like a sunbeam off a mirror. Kron the Withered barely had time to register what was happening before his own spell enveloped him. The evil warlock vanished in a puff of smoke, leaving nothing behind but a pile of ash and Headmaster Aldern's amulet.

The sudden silence in the cavern was deafening.

"We're alive," Dash muttered. Keighlan turned her head and surveyed the scene with one open eye.

Lazzy didn't care. He pulled Gearix close and pressed his lips to hers. She didn't hesitate to shove her tongue right into his mouth. He lurched back in shock and surprise and then went with it. Gearix felt good.

"Kids?" Aldern mumbled. "A little help here?"

— CHAPTER ONE —

G oody's, the most popular dive bar in the ancient neighborhood of Evitankari known as Old Ev, was packed to
bursting with elves celebrating Roger Brooks's victory
against Axzar and the Witch just a few hours prior. It was a tiny,
claustrophobic space to begin with, which meant any single
movement in any direction resulted in a chain of additional
movements spreading outward in all directions like a ripple in
a pond. Conversation wasn't so much a dull roar as a collection
of several dozen screaming competitions struggling mightily to
outdo each other. None of those in attendance cared about the
AM hour, which in polite society is typically considered far too
early to get that intoxicated. Elves and polite society, it turns
out, go together not so much like oil and water but more like a
tomato and a sledgehammer. It's not pretty.

Also not pretty: the expression on Lazzy's face. Dash couldn't
decide if Lazzy looked constipated, utterly depressed, or just
disgusted. He settled on "constipressgusted," took a long
swig from his giant glass stein of cheap swill, and leaned back
against their booth's hard wooden bench to watch the pants-
suited businesswoman doing a keg stand in the corner. Yes,

Goody's allows keg stands—but only on special occasions, like the Pintiri's birthday, Secretary's Day, or, to be honest, most Wednesdays.

"It's like we're not even here," Keighlan, Dash's wife, muttered from beside him. The remains of four extra dirty martinis—strategically ordered all at once for efficiency's sake and subsequently slammed back with the same competence and economy—surrounded her like a tiny glass honor guard. She'd been tracing increasingly malformed figure eights on the skin of Dash's muscular right forearm for the last twenty minutes, a nervous habit that meant she had a problem that required her husband's undivided attention. Dash had decided to ignore her in the hopes that she'd get angry and cause a scene so they could go home already.

"My glass has been empty for ten minutes," Lazzy moaned, his babyface somehow pinching itself left and right and up and down all at the same time. Short and thin as a rail, Lazzy had always made up for his lack of stature with a powerful personality and the sort of can-do attitude that's mostly gone extinct outside of home renovation shows. "We haven't had to buy our own drinks in this town...ever," Lazzy continued.

"Had to happen eventually," Dash said, trying to keep the strain out of his voice. He was glad no one in Goody's was paying them any mind. Adoring fans and would-be hangers-on had been all up in his business for far too long. "We had a good run."

"Doesn't mean we have to like it," Gearix, Lazzy's wife, mused from her spot slumped in the corner. Strands of her wispy red hair stuck oddly in the nooks and crannies of the wall. The splash of freckles that had been a mark of shame in her youth now made Dash's heart flutter. She'd had a single small beer and called it a morning. She'd always been the quiet, introspective one of the group, content to let the other three take the lead and garner all the attention while she worked things out in the background. Dash could tell from the tightness in her lips and the set of her jaw that she was busy at work doing just that.

"We shouldn't have to like it," Lazzy declared with a slight slur. "Eighteen years ago, we—just a precocious quartet of teenagers barely into our third year in the academy—single-handedly thwarted Kron the Withered's attempt to destroy Evitankari. We're heroes! None of these people would even be here without us!"

"We had a good run," Dash repeated. Lazzy could ramble on for hours if no one derailed him, and Dash had an upcoming and urgent appointment with his recliner, his home brew, and a Spurs/Bulls game later that afternoon. "Maybe give it a few days, Laz. That human and his wife and Council of Intelligence Driff are probably just the flavor of the month."

"Or they're next year's model," Gearix said wistfully, "and we're the old junkers on the back lot, ruined by time and depreciation to the point that even the dealership's most desperate salesmen won't bring anyone out to see us."

"I get to be a Mazda Miata," Keighlan replied sleepily. "Remember when we rented one of those in Florida, D?"

This was Dash's chance. "I'm pretty sure that was some sort of Chevy, K." It absolutely wasn't and he knew it.

She blinked at him in surprise. "No, it was a yellow Miata. With leather seats."

Lazzy grabbed the shirt of the nearest patron walking past. "Hey. You know who I am?" The guy looked down at him, scowled, and slid deeper into the crowd.

Dash took another drink from his beer to steel his nerves. "It was a Chevy Camaro," he said bluntly. "Blue."

Keighlan recoiled from him in sloppy drunken horror. "It was not!"

In the corner, Gearix idly traced her finger along a ragged heart carved into the wall.

"It was definitely a Chevy," Dash said.

Lazzy leaned out of the booth and yanked a woman's skirt to get her attention. "Miss, do you know who I am?"

She spun around and slapped him in the face. "Quit it, perv!" She melted away into the masses behind a wall of angry male companions.

"D, I can't believe you! That was definitely a Miata!"

"Chevy."

"And why are you so intent on correcting me in front of our friends?"

"Because you're wrong."

A broad shadow darkened the booth. Dash looked up to find an obese, red-faced elf in an ill-fitting gray business suit had squeezed himself into the narrow space between their table and the three dudes still glowering at Lazzy.

"Do you know who I am?" Lazzy asked.

The newcomer nodded. A few drops of sweat from his broad forehead spattered the table. "I'm familiar with each of you. Lazzy, the headstrong hero with a heart of gold. Gearix, the former ugly duckling who loves Lazzy with all her heart. Keighlan, the energetic overachiever with a solution for every problem." He paused. "And Dash, the sidekick."

Too stunned for words, Dash stared up at the wide elf in dumb shock. Sure, everyone in Evitankari knew their story backward and forward, but few would ever describe his role in such dismissive terms—even if they agreed with that assessment in private.

"And you're Council of Economics Granger," Gearix said coolly. "To what do we owe the pleasure?"

"I'm here on business, of course," Granger replied with a Cheshire Cat grin. "And today's business is that human Pintiri you're all so jealous of."

"We're not jealous!" Lazzy protested. "We just don't want to be forgotten."

"Fuck that," Keighlan slurred. "I'm jealous."

Granger shrugged. "Either way, I believe I can be of assistance."

"How?" Gearix asked, clearly skeptical.

Granger's grin expanded into a double-wide, complete with attached deck. "I have reason to believe the Pintiri's 'defeat' of the demon lord Axzar didn't go exactly as the official story would have us believe."

"I knew it!" Lazzy shouted as if he'd just discovered the secret of cold fusion.

"Dirty humans," Keighlan muttered.

Dash ignored the excited glances bouncing around the table and drained the remainder of his beer as he turned Granger's words over in his mind. *Gee*, he thought angrily, *doesn't all that sound familiar.*